Maya's Last Wish

An Epic Saga of Love & Pain

Maya's Last Wish

Darshan Singh

Published by:
FREEDOM PUBLISHING HOUSE

MAYA'S LAST WISH
by **Darshan Singh**

ISBN: 978-93-93675-61-3

Published by: **Freedom Publishing House**
SCF 32, PHASE 5, MOHALI, PUNJAB, INDIA, 160059

Printed in India

Dedication

This book is dedicated to those who have endured the hardships of love, to those who have felt the profound pain of losing someone dear, and to those who were cherished by a partner who loved them endlessly but could not stay by their side for long. May their memories live on, and may love, in all its depth and beauty, continue to inspire the heart.

About the Author

Darshan Singh is a passionate writer of fiction, non-fiction, and poetry, crafting stories and ideas that leave a lasting impact on people's lives. His fictional works go beyond mere entertainment—they serve as a powerful medium to help readers navigate struggles, setbacks, and hardships. With a deep commitment to storytelling that inspires and empowers, he continues to write with the purpose of motivating individuals across the globe, offering them strength, resilience, and hope through his words.

Inspiration for the Book

The inspiration for this book stems from the author's seven visits to the beautiful country of Malaysia over the past seven years. During these journeys, he has been deeply captivated by Malaysia's rich culture, warm-hearted people, diverse cuisine, and breathtaking landscapes. From its bustling cities to its serene islands, from its vibrant festivals to its deep-rooted traditions, every aspect of this nation has left an indelible mark on his heart.

His continuous exploration and admiration for Malaysia persuaded him to dedicate a novel to this remarkable country. Rather than writing a travel book, he chose to weave Malaysia's greatest treasures into a compelling work of fiction—one that not only transports readers to its stunning destinations, introduces them to its exquisite food, and immerses them in its cultural richness, but also inspires the timeless beauty of love.

Maya Tan Xin Yi was born into a humble Hokkien Chinese family in Malaysia. Unlike many of her peers, she carried a name that stood out—Maya—chosen by her modern-minded parents who believed in breaking away from rigid traditions. Her father, Tan Chee Meng, and her mother, Lim Siew Lan, had always been pragmatic dreamers. They ran a small printing shop in Kuala Lumpur, pouring every ounce of effort into making ends meet, always dreaming of a better future for their only daughter.

From a young age, Maya witnessed her parents' relentless hard work. Their struggles became her motivation, their sacrifices a silent lesson that life was never meant to be easy. While other children played in the neighborhood, she sat at the shop's back corner, poring over schoolbooks, solving math problems, and memorizing English vocabulary from tattered dictionaries. She had no time for distractions—every ounce of her energy was dedicated to securing a future far beyond the narrow streets of her childhood.

Her diligence bore fruit when she earned a prestigious scholarship to study in Scotland, an achievement that was not just hers but a victory for her entire family. The scholarship meant everything—it was her chance to rise beyond the financial hardships, to bring her parents' dreams to life. When the acceptance letter arrived, her mother wept, her father patted her shoulder with quiet pride, and Maya felt the weight of their hopes settle upon her shoulders.

The day she boarded the plane, she carried more than just her luggage. She carried the unspoken promise that their sacrifices would not be in vain. As she stepped onto the cobbled streets of Edinburgh, the crisp foreign air sent a shiver down her spine—a stark contrast to the humid warmth of Kuala Lumpur. Yet, she welcomed it. This was her new beginning, the place where she would carve her own future.

The University of Edinburgh stood before her like a towering monument to knowledge, its ancient stone buildings whispering stories of scholars who had walked these paths long before her. She moved through the halls with purpose, determined to make every moment count. Days turned into weeks, and Maya quickly adapted to the rhythm of university life. Her days were filled with lectures, late-night study sessions, and endless cups of coffee. Every challenge, every obstacle was met with the same determination that had carried her this far.

There was no room for distraction. Or so she thought—until she found herself drawn into a world beyond textbooks, a world of friendships, unexpected emotions, and the kind of longing she never anticipated.

*****

The crisp autumn breeze swept through the sprawling campus of the University of Edinburgh, rustling the scarlet leaves that clung stubbornly to the ancient trees. The grand stone buildings, adorned with ivy creeping up their facades, stood as silent witnesses to the countless stories that unfolded within their walls. Among these stories was one that had just begun—a story of friendship, longing, and an unspoken love that would soon be tested by time and fate.

In a large lecture hall, students filled in, taking their seats in the semicircular rows of wooden desks that faced a vast chalkboard. The room buzzed with the low murmur of conversations, the occasional laughter punctuating the scholarly air. At the front of the hall, Professor Caldwell adjusted his spectacles and shuffled through his notes, preparing for his lecture on cultural anthropology.

Maya leaned against the backrest of her seat, her dark brown eyes scanning the room as she absently twirled a pen between her fingers. She had always found solace in the structured chaos of academia, but today, an ache sat heavy in her chest. She missed Malaysia—its vibrant streets, the scent of *satay* sizzling at roadside stalls, the rhythmic hum of life that never seemed to pause. The cold, gray skies of Scotland only deepened her yearning for home.

Beside her, Aaryan slid into his seat, setting down his laptop and offering her a warm smile. "You're looking extra thoughtful today. Lost in another world?"

Maya sighed, resting her chin on her palm. "More like lost in memories. I miss Malaysia so much. The food, the weather, the people... everything."

Aaryan chuckled, nudging her lightly. "Well, I wouldn't know. Never been there. But from the way you describe it, it sounds like paradise."

"It is," Maya said wistfully. "You should visit sometime. I'd give you the grand tour."

Their conversation was interrupted as the lecture began. Professor Caldwell cleared his throat and addressed the class, his deep voice carrying effortlessly across the room. "Today, we'll be discussing cultural identity and the impact of globalization on personal heritage. As we explore this, I want each of you to consider your own background, how has your culture shaped your identity? How has living in a different country changed your perception of it?"

Maya straightened slightly; her interest piqued. She often found herself reflecting on these very questions. The longer she stayed in the UK, the more she realized how deeply rooted her identity was in Malaysia. The flavors, the traditions, the unspoken rules of home were all a part of her, no matter how far she traveled.

As the lecture progressed, another voice joined the discussion. "Sometimes, leaving home makes you appreciate it even more. I never thought much about my Indian heritage until I moved here," said Rohan, a fellow student with an easygoing demeanor and an ever-present grin.

Aaryan nodded in agreement. "Same here. Being away from home really puts things in perspective."

Professor Caldwell gestured toward Maya. "And what about you, Miss Tan? How has your experience in the UK influenced your view of your cultural identity?"

Maya hesitated for a moment before answering. "I think it has made me realize how much of my identity is tied to Malaysia. When I was there, I was always busy studying, working, making plans for the future. I never stopped to appreciate the little things, like a simple meal at a hawker stall or the way the city lights reflect on the river at night. But now, those are the things I miss the most."

The professor nodded approvingly. "That's an insightful observation. Often, distance grants us clarity."

After class, Maya, Aaryan, and Rohan strolled across the campus courtyard, the cobblestone path slippery from an earlier drizzle. They found a spot on a stone bench beneath a towering oak tree, where they often gathered after lectures to unwind.

"You really do talk about Malaysia a lot," Aaryan teased, nudging Maya with his elbow. "I think half of my bucket list now consists of places you've mentioned."

Maya grinned. "Good! Maybe one day you'll actually visit."

"One day," Aaryan echoed, unaware that in the years to come, he would find himself drawn to Malaysia in search of his love.

As they sat there, a fourth figure approached—a young woman with ginger hair and an air of effortless confidence. "Mind if I join?" she asked, flashing a bright smile.

"Of course, Lily!" Rohan said, scooting over to make space.

Lily, an exchange student from Canada, had a knack for making friends wherever she went. She sat down beside them, stretching her legs out. "So, what's today's topic of discussion?"

"Cultural identity and how Maya is secretly a tourism ambassador for Malaysia," Aaryan quipped.

Maya laughed. "I can't help it. It's who I am."

Lily's eyes twinkled with curiosity. "You know, I'd love to visit Malaysia too. What's the first place you'd take us if we all went?"

Maya didn't hesitate. "Georgetown in Penang. It's a mix of history, street art, and amazing food. You'd love it."

As they talked and laughed, the chill of the Scottish air seemed to fade, replaced by the warmth of shared stories and dreams of future adventures. It was in moments like these that Maya felt most at home, even in a foreign land. And it was in moments like these that Aaryan, though he didn't voice it yet, began to realize just how much Maya had come to mean to him.

Unbeknownst to them all, life had already begun weaving its intricate web, setting the stage for a bond that would transcend borders, time, and the inevitability of fate.

Maya and Aaryan's friendship deepened over the next few months. They often found themselves studying together in the library, lingering over cups of coffee at the student café, and debating everything from history to pop culture. Maya's spirit and determination impressed Aaryan, though she never spoke much about her struggles.

One evening, as they sat under the dim glow of fairy lights outside the university café, Aaryan casually remarked, "You just keep bragging about Malaysia. What's so special about it?"

Maya smiled, her eyes sparkling. "You'll see when you come there. One day, I'll show you everything—every city, every hidden gem, every dish that makes Malaysia what it is."

There was a quiet sincerity in her voice, and Aaryan felt a flicker of curiosity stir within him. He didn't realize it yet, but her words had planted a seed, one that would soon lead him to a journey he never expected to take.

*****

The sun had barely risen when Maya's phone buzzed violently against the wooden bedside table. It was an unfamiliar number. She slowly reached for it, rubbing the sleep from her eyes.

"Hello?" Her voice was hoarse from exhaustion. There was silence on the other end, followed by a heavy sigh. Then, a voice spoke, unfamiliar yet filled with urgency.

"Is this Maya Tan?"

"Yes, who's this?"

A pause. Then the words came like a hammer to her chest.

"This is Inspector Rahim from the Kuala Lumpur Police Department. I'm... I'm sorry to inform you that your parents were involved in a bus accident late last night."

Maya's breath caught in her throat. "W-What?" she stammered, already feeling her heart begin to race.

"There was a collision with a truck. Your parents... they didn't survive." The world tilted. The walls of her tiny dorm room seemed to close in, and the voice on the phone faded into an incomprehensible blur.

"No... no, that can't be," Maya whispered, gripping the bedsheet with trembling fingers.

"I'm very sorry for your loss."

She barely remembered the rest of the call—something about paperwork, next of kin, and a funeral. But none of it mattered. Her parents were gone. A scream built up inside her chest, but it wouldn't come out.

Instead, she sat frozen, the phone slipping from her fingers onto the bed. For what felt like hours, she sat there, staring at nothing. The room was silent except for the faint ticking of her clock, an eerie contrast to the storm raging inside her. It was Lily who found her first.

Maya hadn't shown up for class that morning, and her phone had gone silent. Concerned, Lily had come to check on her. The moment she saw Maya sitting there, pale and unmoving, she knew something was terribly wrong.

"Maya?" she called softly, stepping into the room. There was no response from Maya.

She hesitated for a moment before walking closer. That's when she saw the phone lying on the bed, the call log still open. And then she saw Maya's eyes—red-rimmed, vacant, staring at the wall like she wasn't really there.

“Oh my God...” Lily whispered. She crouched in front of Maya, placing a gentle hand on her knee. “Maya, talk to me. What happened?”

When Maya finally spoke, her voice was hollow. “They're gone.”

“Who's gone?”

“My parents.”

Lily's breath hitched. “Oh, Maya...”

Maya squeezed her eyes shut, as if trying to block out reality. “They were in an accident. I... I didn't even say goodbye.”

Lily's throat tightened. She didn't know what to say. No words could fix this. Instead, she pulled Maya into a hug. For a long time, Maya didn't react. Then, slowly, she broke down. A choked sob escaped her lips, followed by another. And then the dam burst. Lily held her as she shook, her cries muffled against her shoulder.

By the time Aaryan and Rohan heard the news, it had spread across the campus. No one knew the full details, only that Maya had lost both her parents in a tragic accident. Aaryan wasted no time. He ran to Maya's dorm, finding the door already open. Inside, he saw Lily sitting beside Maya on the bed, rubbing slow circles on her back. Maya's eyes were swollen, her body curled in on itself as if trying to disappear.

Aaryan gulped nervously, stepping inside. "Maya..."

She didn't look up.

Aaryan had never been good with words in moments like these. What could he say? That everything would be, okay? That time would heal her pain? It would all be a lie. Instead, he sat beside her, carefully placing a hand on her shoulder.

"I'm here," he murmured. "Whatever you need."

Maya let out a shaky breath but didn't respond. The room was silent for a long time, except for her uneven breathing. Later that evening, Rohan and Lily sat with Aaryan in the library, their books forgotten.

"She has no family left," Lily said softly. "Just distant relatives, but none close enough to help."

Aaryan frowned. "And she doesn't have money to fly back, does she?"

Rohan shook his head. "She was on a full government scholarship. Every penny she had went into food and rent. Even if she sells everything, she won't have enough for a last-minute ticket to Malaysia." The weight of the situation sank heavily between them.

Lily bit her lip. "We need to do something."

Aaryan took a deep breath. "We will."

That night, Aaryan sat in his tiny apartment, staring at his phone. He had one option left. He called his father. The phone rang for a few seconds before a warm voice answered.

"Aaryan! Son, how are you?"

Aaryan hesitated. His parents were middle-class—comfortable, but not wealthy. Asking for money wasn't easy.

"Papa... I need some money," he said slowly.

There was a pause. "How much?"

"A thousand pounds."

After a moment of silence. "Aaryan, that's a lot. What's going on?"

Aaryan clenched his jaw. He couldn't tell them the real reason. His father would worry too much, and he might not even agree.

"It's for a university project," he lied. "A research trip. I need to book flights."

His father sighed. "This is unexpected... but if you need it, we'll manage."

Guilt churned in Aaryan's stomach. But when he thought of Maya, lost and helpless, he knew he had no choice. By the end of the next day, Rohan, Lily, and several other friends had pooled together what they could. Aaryan contributed the most, using the money from his parents. That evening, they gathered in Maya's room. She looked up at them, dull eyes and lifeless. Aaryan stepped forward, holding out an envelope.

"Here."

Maya frowned. "What's this?"

"A ticket home."

She blinked, not understanding.

"We got it for you," Lily said gently.

Maya's lips parted in disbelief. "You... you bought me a ticket?"

Rohan shrugged. "Of course. You need to be in Malaysia right now."

Tears welled in her eyes again, but this time, they weren't just from grief. They were from love, the kind that came from knowing she wasn't alone. She looked at Aaryan. He simply smiled.

"You always said you missed Malaysia," he murmured. "I never imagined it happening like this, but... you're going home, Maya."

Maya choked back a sob, nodding. Then, for the first time in days, she leaned forward and hugged him. After a moment, she pulled away and left.

*****

The cold winds of Edinburgh hadn't changed, but Maya Tan had. Two weeks had passed since she had left for Malaysia, and now she was back, walking through the university gates with an unreadable expression. Her steps were quick, purposeful, as though she was racing against time itself. The grief that had weighed down her shoulders before was still there, but it had been buried beneath something stronger—determination.

Her return to Malaysia had been a blur of sorrow and responsibilities. Her relatives had stepped in immediately, arranging the funeral with care and ensuring that all traditions were honored. They guided her through the rituals, offering their quiet strength when she needed it the most. Even in the midst of her loss, she was grateful for them.

In the days following the funeral, Maya discovered that her parents had left behind a substantial amount of savings in a bank account—money they had quietly set aside for her future. That final act of love, their silent sacrifice, overwhelmed her with emotion. It was enough to sustain her for another three to four years, ensuring that she wouldn't have to struggle financially. With a heavy heart and a silent thank you to her parents, she used part of that money to book her flight back to Scotland.

Now, as she stepped back onto campus, she knew she had no choice but to move forward. She had come too far, sacrificed too much to falter now. This was her parents' dream, and she would not let it slip away.

Aaryan noticed her the moment she stepped onto campus. She stood near the library, wrapped in a thick coat, her long black hair tied in a ponytail. There was a quiet resolve in her posture, a steadiness that hadn't been there before. The girl who had once broken down in his arms, overwhelmed by grief, was gone. In her place was someone who had endured, who had buried her pain beneath an unyielding resolve. And yet, as he watched her, he couldn't help but wonder—had she truly healed, or had she simply learned how to hide the wounds?

"Maya," he called out.

She turned, her lips parting in a soft smile. "Aaryan."

It was the same voice, but there was something sharper in it, something more distant.

Aaryan walked up to her. "Welcome back. How... how are you?"

"I'm good." Her answer came too quickly, too firmly.

He observed her closely. She looked the same, but there was energy in her that hadn't been there before—a drive, an intensity. It was like she had returned with a mission. Lily and Rohan arrived a moment later, their faces lit up as they saw Maya.

"Maya!" Lily exclaimed, pulling her into a tight hug. "We missed you so much."

Maya smiled, returning the hug, but there was still a distance in her warmth, as though she had built a wall around herself.

"How was Malaysia?" Rohan asked cautiously.

Maya took a deep breath. "It was... difficult. But I did what I had to do."

There was silence for a moment before she continued, her voice unwavering. "Now, I'm back. And I'm going to make sure my parents' struggles weren't in vain. No more wasting time."

Aaryan frowned slightly. "Maya, you don't have to prove anything—"

She cut him off with a small shake of her head. "I do, Aaryan. I really do." And just like that, the conversation ended.

Within days, Maya threw herself into her studies with an intensity that surprised everyone. She spent hours in the library, scribbling notes, revising lectures, preparing for exams that were still months away. While others took breaks to relax or unwind at cafés, Maya pushed forward relentlessly.

Rohan leaned back in his chair one evening, stretching his arms. "Okay, that's it. I'm done. No more studying for today."

Aaryan nodded in agreement. "Same here. My brain is officially fried."

They both turned to Maya, expecting her to pack up as well. Instead, she was still bent over her book, eyes scanning the pages as she jotted down notes.

"Maya," Aaryan called, but there was no reply.

He sighed. "Maya." Still getting no response.

Finally, he reached over and pulled her notebook away.

She looked up, startled. "What the hell, Aaryan?"

"You've been at this for six hours straight. Come on, let's grab some coffee."

Maya shook her head, reaching for her notebook. "I don't have time for coffee."

Aaryan didn't give it back. "You don't have time to live either, apparently."

She sighed in frustration. "Aaryan, I'm not like you. I don't have a family to support me. I don't have time to waste."

His jaw tightened. "You think I waste time?"

She exhaled, rubbing her temples. "That's not what I meant."

Aaryan leaned forward, his voice softer now. "Maya, I get it. You want to succeed; you want to honor your parents. But you're not a machine. You need to breathe."

Maya shook her head. "I'll breathe when I've made something of myself."

Aaryan exhaled, realizing that arguing wouldn't change her mind. He had always believed in balance—working hard, but also making time for music, movies, and late-night conversations over coffee. But Maya... she was relentless.

One afternoon, they were sitting in the student lounge when the topic came up again.

"I swear, you're the only person I know who never stops working," Aaryan teased, taking a sip of his coffee.

Maya smirked. "And you're the only person I know who doesn't take life seriously enough."

"I take life seriously," he argued. "I just don't believe in running so fast that you forget to enjoy the journey."

Maya leaned back, crossing her arms. "Enjoying the journey is a privilege, Aaryan. Not all of us can afford it."

Aaryan sighed. "And what happens when you finally achieve everything you want? When you have all the money, all the success? Then what?"

"Then I'll be free," she said simply.

"To do what?"

She hesitated. "To see the world. To visit every city in Malaysia, just like I always dreamed."

Aaryan smiled. "You don't have to wait for success to do that."

She scoffed. "You sound like one of those motivational speakers. 'Live in the moment.' 'Money isn't everything.'" She shook her head. "That's easy for you to say, Aaryan. You don't know what it's like to have nothing."

His expression darkened slightly. "You think I don't understand struggle?"

Maya said quickly, "I didn't mean it like that."

There was a brief silence before Aaryan spoke again, his voice gentle. "Maya, I just don't want you to look back one day and realize you never really lived."

She looked at him for a long time, something unreadable in her eyes. Then, she smiled faintly.

"I'll live, Aaryan," she said. "Just not yet."

No matter how focused Maya became, her dream never faded. At night, when the library was empty and the world was quiet, she would close her eyes and picture it—standing on the beaches of Langkawi, wandering the streets of Malacca, tasting street food in Penang. She would see every corner of Malaysia, the way she had always dreamed. Someday, but for now, she had work to do. And nothing, not even Aaryan's gentle reminders—would slow her down.

*****

The end of university came faster than any of them had expected. One moment, they were first-year students trying to navigate their way through a foreign country, struggling with assignments, late-night study sessions, and endless cups of coffee. And now, suddenly, they were standing at the threshold of their future, ready to step into the real world.

Maya Tan had done what she always set out to do. She had topped the final exams. It wasn't a surprise to anyone. From the moment she had returned to Edinburgh after her parents' tragedy, Maya had thrown herself into her studies with an intensity that had left everyone in awe. She had been unstoppable—absorbing knowledge like a sponge, acing every test, outshining even the brightest minds in her class.

But somewhere in those final weeks, she had also begun to ease back into life. The wounds of her loss didn't heal completely, but the sharp edges dulled, and she started smiling more, laughing more. And Aaryan—he had been there through it all.

One evening, a few days before graduation, Aaryan and Maya sat on the rooftop of their dormitory, their legs dangling over the edge as they watched the golden hues of the sunset paint the sky. It had become their spot—an escape from the noise, a place where they could talk freely.

"I knew you'd top," Aaryan said, glancing at Maya. "It was never even a question."

Maya smirked. "Are you saying you weren't even competing with me?"

"Compete with you?" Aaryan scoffed, placing a hand on his chest in mock offense. "I was just trying to survive in this place. But you—Maya Tan—were always meant to win."

She chuckled, shaking her head. "It's not about winning, Aaryan. It's about getting what I've always wanted. This degree, this career... it's just the beginning."

Aaryan watched her closely, his eyes filled with contemplation. "And then what? After you've worked hard and achieved everything, what comes next?"

Maya turned her gaze to the horizon. "Then, I live my dream."

He grinned. "Ah yes, the famous Malaysia tour. The one you keep advertising."

Maya laughed, nudging him with her shoulder. "I wasn't advertising! I was just... sharing my love for my country."

"More like obsessing over it," Aaryan teased. "Seriously, Maya, if I had a dollar for every time you talked about Malaysia, I'd be a billionaire by now."

She tilted her head, smiling. "And you still haven't seen it with your own eyes. That's your fault."

Aaryan shrugged. "Well, the invitation was never serious, was it?"

Maya's smile faded slightly, and she turned to face him fully. "Of course, it was serious. I told you before—I'd show you everything. Every city, every street, every festival. You just have to come."

There was something in her voice, something real. It wasn't just a casual invitation anymore; it was a promise.

Aaryan nodded slowly. "Alright then. One day, I'll come. And you better keep your word."

Maya extended her pinky finger toward him. "Promise me."

Aaryan chuckled, linking his pinky with hers. "Promise."

Graduation came and went in a blur of ceremonies, photographs, and farewell parties. And then, just like that, everyone started moving in different directions. Maya landed a job in one of Malaysia's top corporate firms, exactly as she had planned. She was set to leave within a week after graduation, eager to start her new life. Aaryan, on the other hand, had chosen a slightly different path. He had secured a job with an international firm based in London—one that offered stability and growth, but not the relentless hustle that Maya had signed up for.

The night before Maya left, they met for one last time at their favorite café near campus. The place was quieter than usual, the late hours thinning out the crowd.

"So, this is it," Aaryan said, stirring his coffee. "The last time I see Maya Tan before she turns into some high-profile corporate boss who's too busy for her old friends."

Maya rolled her eyes. "I will always have time for my friends."

Aaryan raised an eyebrow. "We'll see."

She leaned forward. “We’ll talk, Aaryan. We’ll meet again. And don’t forget your promise—you’re coming to Malaysia.”

He smiled. “I won’t forget. Just don’t get too busy and disappear.”

Maya hesitated for a moment before saying, “Even if I do, you’ll remind me, right?”

Aaryan gave her a knowing look. “Always.”

They clinked their coffee mugs together, sealing yet another unspoken promise. Both had become great friends, their bond growing stronger over the years. Yet, as they sat there, they couldn’t ignore the weight of parting. Neither voiced it, but inside, they both felt the quiet ache of farewell. They were thinking not only about what lay ahead in life but also about the moments they would leave behind—late-night study sessions, campus walks, endless conversations. College had shaped them, given them memories that would last a lifetime. And now, it was time to move on.

*****

The moment Maya stepped into the tall glass building of her new office in Kuala Lumpur, she knew this was what she had worked for. The energy, the ambition, the drive—everything here moved at the speed she had always craved. Days turned into weeks, and weeks into months. Maya rose through the ranks quickly, impressing her seniors with her efficiency and determination. She worked late nights, attended networking events, and immersed herself completely in the corporate world.

At first, she kept in touch with her friends from college. The occasional messages, the video calls. But as time passed, the calls became less frequent, the messages shorter. The only person she still talked to somewhat regularly was Aaryan. Their conversations were no longer as long as they used to be, but they still checked in on each other.

One evening, Maya's phone rang while she was sitting in her high-rise apartment, going through some reports. Seeing Aaryan's name on the screen, she smiled.

"Look who's finally calling," she answered.

"Hey, big-shot corporate queen," Aaryan teased. "Too busy for us common folks?"

Maya laughed. "I could say the same about you, Mr. London."

"Can't argue with that," he admitted. "So, how's life in the fast lane?"

Maya leaned back in her chair. "It's everything I expected. Busy, exciting, exhausting."

Aaryan was quiet for a moment. "Do you ever stop to breathe, Maya?"

She sighed. "You sound just like you did when we were in university."

"That's because you still haven't changed," he said. "You're still running like you have something to prove."

Maya twirled a pen between her fingers. "Maybe I do."

Aaryan's voice softened. "And what about Malaysia? Have you taken time to actually enjoy it?"

She hesitated. "I... haven't had time yet."

He chuckled. "The great Maya Tan, who spent years convincing me to visit Malaysia, hasn't even explored it herself?"

Maya smiled faintly. "I will. Soon."

Aaryan didn't push her further, but she could hear the quiet concern in his voice.

Before they hung up, he reminded her, "Don't forget our promise."

Maya closed her eyes. "I won't."

Deep down, she felt herself slipping away from the girl who once longed to bring her friends to Malaysia, to show them the place that meant everything to her. As the months passed, life kept pulling Maya and Aaryan in different directions. She became increasingly absorbed in her career; her time stretched thin. Yet, no matter how busy she was, every now and then, she would glance at her phone, read Aaryan's last message, and smile. She hadn't forgotten the promise—and neither had he. One day, she knew, he would come to Malaysia, and she would be there, waiting. Or at least, that's what she told herself.

*****

The lights of Kuala Lumpur's skyline shimmered through the windows of Maya's high-rise office. It was nearly midnight, yet the corporate tower remained alive. Employees bent over their desks, the soft hum of keyboards, and the occasional murmur of late-night calls. Maya sat at her desk, her face lit by the cold blue glow of her laptop, scanning financial reports with the precision of someone accustomed to running on little sleep. This was her life now—endless work, persistent ambition, and the pursuit of success. Her phone vibrated beside her. She barely glanced at the screen before sighing.

Aaryan. Again.

She hesitated for a moment before answering. "Aaryan, it's late. What's up?"

A familiar voice, filled with warmth yet laced with concern, responded. "That's what I was about to ask you. Do you ever stop working, Maya?"

She smiled faintly but didn't look away from the screen. "Not today. Big project."

Aaryan sighed on the other end. "You always say that. When's the last time you actually took a break? Spend time outside your office? Or have you forgotten that you promised someone a tour of Malaysia?"

Maya giggled lightly. "I didn't forget. I just—"

"You just keep pushing it back," Aaryan interrupted. "How many times have I asked? Five? Ten?"

Maya leaned back in her chair, massaging her forehead.

"Aaryan, I'm really busy right now. I can't just drop everything and take a vacation."

"I'm not asking for a vacation. I'm asking you to keep a promise," he said, his tone softer now. "You always talked about showing me your country. I thought you'd be excited about it."

She felt a pang of guilt but pushed it aside. "I will. Just... not right now. Once this project is over."

Aaryan exhaled sharply. "That's exactly what you said last time. And the time before that."

Maya closed her eyes. She knew he was right. But she also knew she wasn't ready to slow down.

"Aaryan," she said, keeping her voice steady, "I'll call you later, okay? I really need to finish this."

There was a pause, and then, with quiet understanding, he simply said, "Alright, Maya. Take care."

She hung up, placing the phone down with more force than necessary, as if silencing the voice of reason that Aaryan always seemed to be in her life. As Maya packed up to leave, her office door creaked open, and a familiar figure entered—Fatimah, her closest friend at work.

Fatimah was ten years older, a woman with kind eyes and a heart as vast as the sky. She carried a small container in her hands, setting it down on Maya's desk.

"I knew you wouldn't eat," Fatimah said, crossing her arms. "So, I brought you dinner from home."

Maya glanced at the food; her exhaustion momentarily replaced by warmth. “You really don’t have to do this, Fatimah.”

“I do,” Fatimah said firmly. “Because you won’t do it for yourself.”

Maya sighed, opening the container to find a warm meal—home-cooked nasi lemak, the rich aroma instantly making her stomach rumble.

“You’re spoiling me,” Maya said with a smile.

Fatimah smirked. “Someone has to. You live like a robot.”

Maya chuckled, but the words stung because they weren’t untrue.

As Maya ate, Fatimah sat across from her. “Aaryan called again?” she asked knowingly.

Maya rolled her eyes. “You’re worse than my mother.”

Fatimah shrugged. “If I were your mother, I’d drag you out of this office myself and make you live a little.”

Maya stabbed a piece of chicken with her fork. “I will. After this project.”

Fatimah groaned, shaking her head. “You’ve been saying that for years, Maya. You’ve built walls around yourself. You work, you go home, you sleep, and then you repeat. Where’s the life in that?”

Maya didn’t answer immediately. Instead, she focused on her food.

Fatimah softened. “Maya, you’re successful, yes. But at what cost? Do you have anyone to celebrate with?”

Maya opened her mouth to protest but found herself at a loss for words.

Fatimah leaned forward. "You work so hard to earn a good life, but you're forgetting to live it."

Maya swallowed hard, avoiding her friend's gaze. "I'm fine, Fatimah."

"No, you're not," Fatimah said gently. "And Aaryan knows it too. That's why he keeps calling."

Maya replied, "He just doesn't get it. I have responsibilities now."

Fatimah shook her head. "No, Maya. He gets it more than anyone. That's why he's the only one still here, still trying to pull you out of this cycle."

Maya barely acknowledged Fatimah's words, letting them drift past her like a breeze she refused to feel.

Days turned into weeks, and the same conversations kept happening. Aaryan would call, Maya would push him away. One evening, Aaryan's voice carried a different tone—one laced with frustration.

"Maya, I'm done asking," he said. "I've been patient. I've waited. But you keep choosing work over everything else."

Maya clenched her jaw. "It's not a choice, Aaryan. It's my life."

"No, Maya. It's just an excuse." The words landed heavy between them, the silence that followed stretching like a void.

"I'm happy, Aaryan," Maya finally said, though the words felt hollow.

Aaryan let out a short, bitter laugh. “Are you? Really? Or are you just convincing yourself that you are?”

Maya pressed her fingers to her forehead, rubbing it as if to ease the tension building inside her. “Aaryan, I don’t have time for this.”

“That’s exactly the problem,” he said softly. “You don’t have time for anything that truly matters.”

"Maya swallowed against the dryness in her throat. 'I’ll call you later,' she murmured, though she wasn’t even sure if she meant it."

Aaryan’s voice was quiet. “Sure, Maya. But I already know you won’t.”

The call ended, and Maya sat there, staring at her phone, an unfamiliar weight settling in her chest.

That night, as she sat in her apartment, overlooking the city she had conquered, a hollow feeling crept in. Her life was everything she had dreamed of—money, status, success. Yet, it felt... incomplete. She had no family left, only a handful of friends, and the one person who had always been there for her was slipping away.

Maya sighed, rubbing her face.

Maybe Aaryan was right. Maybe Fatimah was right. Maybe, just maybe, she had been running so hard toward success that she had forgotten what she was actually running for. But the real problem was that she didn’t know how to stop. She didn’t know how to live beyond the chase. And she was afraid that by the time she figured it out, she’d have lost everything that truly mattered.

*****

The towering glass-and-steel structure of Maya's office gleamed under the Kuala Lumpur sun, reflecting the ambition and ruthlessness that thrived within its walls. The company she worked for was one of the top firms in Malaysia, a powerhouse of corporate success—but beneath its polished surface, the work culture was anything but welcoming.

Maya had always been ambitious, ruthless in her pursuit of success. But she hadn't anticipated just how toxic the environment could be. It was late afternoon when Maya entered the conference room, files neatly arranged in her arms, her expression composed. A major project was up for discussion, and Maya had prepared thoroughly. She took her usual seat next to Fatimah, who gave her a reassuring glance.

Across the table sat Daryl and Natasha—two senior employees who had been in the firm long before Maya arrived. They had never hidden their resentment toward her, whether it was because she had climbed the ranks too quickly or because she outperformed them at every turn.

As Maya began her presentation, explaining the financial projections for the upcoming quarter, she noticed the dismissive glances exchanged between Daryl and Natasha.

"This strategy might work in theory," Daryl interrupted, leaning back in his chair, arms crossed. "But in practice? I doubt it. We don't need big, ambitious plans. We need something realistic."

Maya kept her expression neutral. "The numbers suggest otherwise. If we follow this structure, we could see a revenue increase of at least 15% in the next quarter."

Natasha smirked. "Oh, look at that. The company's rising star has everything figured out." Her voice dripped with sarcasm. "Tell me, Maya, do you think experience means nothing? Because we've seen plenty of these 'ambitious' ideas crash and burn."

Maya clenched her jaw. She was used to this—being undermined, being made to feel like she didn't belong.

"I value experience," Maya replied evenly. "But I also believe in data. And the data shows that innovation leads to growth. If we don't evolve, we stagnate."

Daryl scoffed. "Big words for someone so new."

Before Maya could respond, Fatimah cut in. "Maya has a point. The industry is changing, and we need to adapt. Maybe instead of dismissing the idea outright, we analyze it properly?"

A tense silence followed. Eventually, the manager, Mr. Lim, cleared his throat. "Let's take a deeper look at Maya's proposal before making any decisions."

The meeting continued, but Maya felt the weight of Natasha's glare on her the entire time.

As they left the conference room, Fatimah nudged her. "Don't let them get to you."

Maya sighed. "They'll never accept me, will they?"

Fatimah smiled knowingly. "They don't have to. You're here for a reason, and your success will always bother people who aren't willing to work as hard as you."

Maya nodded, but deep down, she wondered how long she could keep fighting these silent battles. A week later, Maya found herself on the receiving end of another office betrayal. She had been working tirelessly on a client proposal, one that could bring a significant deal to the company. She had shared her ideas with a colleague, Jason, whom she had thought was supportive. But when the day of the presentation arrived, Jason stood before the board and presented Maya's ideas as his own.

Maya sat in stunned silence as he laid out the exact points, she had spent weeks developing. Every strategy, every statistic—word for word, it was her work. She exchanged a glancc with Fatimah, who gave her a look of disbelief.

When the presentation ended, the board members applauded Jason's 'brilliant insights.'

After the meeting, Maya confronted him. "You used my work," she said, her voice steady but firm.

Jason said, laughing, "Relax, Maya. We're on the same team. It's all about the company, isn't it?"

Maya clenched her fists. "It's about integrity."

Jason shrugged. "Grow up. This is how things work here."

Maya felt a burning frustration in her chest. It wasn't the first time she had experienced betrayal in the corporate world, and she knew it wouldn't be the last.

That night, she called Aaryan.

Aaryan picked up after the first ring. "You sound exhausted," he said immediately.

Maya let out a deep breath. "I am."

"What happened this time?"

Maya took a deep breath. "Jason stole my proposal and presented it as his own."

Aaryan was silent for a moment before saying, "I swear, if I ever visit your office, I'll have a word with him."

Maya chuckled despite herself. "And what would you say?"

"That he's a coward who can't come up with his own ideas."

Maya smiled but then exhaled. "I just don't understand, Aaryan. Why is it so hard to find honest people in the corporate world?"

Aaryan's voice was calm. "Because ambition blinds people. Not everyone has the same ethics as you."

Maya leaned back on her couch. "I'm just tired of it all. The politics, the competition, the constant need to prove myself."

Aaryan listened patiently, as he always did.

"You should stop taking it all so seriously," he said after a pause. "You work hard, Maya. But don't let this job take everything from you."

Maya scoffed. "And what do you suggest? That I quit and go live in the mountains?"

Aaryan chuckled. "Not exactly. But at least find something outside of work. Something that makes you happy."

Maya hesitated. "I have you to talk to. That makes me happy."

There was a beat of silence before Aaryan said, "You know I'll always be here."

Maya smiled gently. "I know."

As the weeks passed, Maya continued to climb the corporate ladder, but the loneliness never faded. She still called Aaryan every few days, telling him about her victories, her struggles, and the toxic office politics. Aaryan never interrupted. He simply listened, offering advice when needed, but mostly just being there for her. One night, after a particularly long day, Maya called him again.

"I got promoted," she said.

Aaryan grinned. "That's amazing, Maya!"

Maya hesitated. "Yeah... I should be happy, right?"

Aaryan's smile faded slightly. "You don't sound happy."

Maya mumbled. "I just feel... tired. Like no matter how much I achieve, it's never enough."

Aaryan's voice was gentle. "That's because you're chasing something that has no finish line. Success is great, Maya. But it shouldn't be your entire world."

Maya closed her eyes. "Maybe you're right."

"I usually am," he said playfully.

She chuckled. "You're so full of yourself."

Aaryan taunted. "And yet, you still call me every day."

Maya smirked. "Shut up, Aaryan."

As they laughed, Maya felt a small sense of relief. Despite the toxicity, the betrayals, and the exhausting demands of her job, she had at least one thing that remained constant—Aaryan. And maybe, just maybe, that was enough.

*****

The morning sun cast a golden glow over the Kuala Lumpur skyline as Maya walked into the office with an unusual sense of excitement. She had just closed a major deal for the company, and today was the day she would be formally recognized for her contribution. Dressed in a crisp white blouse and a tailored skirt, she radiated confidence. Her dark eyes gleamed with determination, and a rare, genuine smile graced her lips.

Fatimah, standing near the coffee machine, noticed her immediately. "Look at you," she said, pouring coffee into her cup. "You're actually smiling in the morning."

Maya gushed. "It's a big day. I deserve to be happy once in a while, don't I?"

Fatimah cautioned, "Of course. Just don't let them make you work even harder after this."

Maya waved off the concern. "I'll be fine, Fatimah. Hard work has never scared me."

Fatimah sighed, watching as Maya took her coffee and headed to her desk. She knew Maya too well. The girl never stopped pushing herself. She worked longer hours than anyone else, skipped meals, barely slept, and seemed to live only for work. Fatimah had warned her multiple times, but Maya always laughed it off. Today, however, Fatimah had a strange feeling in her gut. The morning passed in a flurry of meetings, emails, and congratulations. Maya was at her peak, responding to messages, making decisions, and leading discussions. By lunchtime, she felt a slight headache creeping in but ignored it, as she always did.

By late afternoon, her headache had intensified, and her vision blurred slightly. She stood up from her desk, intending to go to the breakroom for water, but before she could take a step—the world spun. The sound of her colleagues' voices faded. Her legs buckled, and she collapsed to the floor. In the next moment, everything went dark. The office erupted into chaos.

"Maya!" someone shouted.

Fatimah was the first to reach her, dropping to her knees and shaking Maya's shoulders. "Maya, wake up! Maya!"

Jason ran to call security, and Natasha, despite her usual hostility, grabbed her phone. "I'm calling an ambulance."

The minutes stretched unbearably long as Maya lay unconscious on the floor. Fatimah held her hand tightly, whispering prayers under her breath. Sirens wailed in the distance, growing louder until paramedics rushed in. Voices overlapped—urgent, hurried—before strong hands lifted Maya onto a stretcher.

The sterile white walls of the hospital swam into Maya's vision as she slowly regained consciousness. Her body felt heavy, her throat dry, and an IV line was attached to her hand. She blinked a few times, trying to make sense of her surroundings. The faint beeping of machines filled the room.

"Maya."

She turned her head slightly and saw Fatimah sitting beside her, eyes filled with worry.

"You collapsed in the office," Fatimah explained gently. "They rushed you here. The doctor said you were severely exhausted. Lack of sleep, stress, dehydration—all of it."

Maya stammered. "I... don't remember much."

Fatimah said, "Of course, you don't. You've been running on empty for months. Your body finally gave out."

Maya tried to sit up, but Fatimah pushed her back gently. "No. You need to rest."

Maya groaned. "I think I'm fine now."

Fatimah gave her a sharp look. "You gave us a real scare, Maya."

Maya fell silent.

Fatimah continued, voice softer but firm. "You need to start taking care of yourself. You can't keep working like a machine."

Maya turned her gaze to the ceiling. She had always prided herself on her strength. But today, her body had betrayed her. Or had she betrayed her body?

A couple of hours later, the doctor entered the room, flipping through Maya's medical chart. He was an older man with a kind but stern face.

"You're lucky," he said. "This could have been worse. You need rest, hydration, and proper nutrition. You're running your body beyond its limits, and that's dangerous."

Maya nodded weakly. "Can I go home?"

The doctor sighed. “We’ll discharge you in the evening, but you need to take at least a few days off work.”

Maya didn’t respond.

Fatimah answered for her. “Don’t worry, doctor. I’ll make sure she takes care of herself.”

The doctor gave Maya one last assessing look before exiting.

Fatimah crossed her arms. “Now, are you going to listen?”

Maya gave a small, tiring smile. “I’ll try.”

Fatimah rolled her eyes. “That’s not good enough, but I suppose it’s a start.”

A few days later, Maya returned to the office. She walked in with her usual confidence, yet something felt different. She still worked hard, still pushed herself, but exhaustion clung to her like a shadow. And then there was the headache, it never truly left. By mid-afternoon, she pressed her fingers to her temples and closed her eyes for a moment, trying to push through the lingering fatigue.

Fatimah appeared beside her desk. “Headache again?”

Maya sighed. “Yeah.”

Fatimah placed a small lunchbox in front of her. “Eat. You probably haven’t eaten properly.”

Maya looked at her in surprise. “You brought food?”

Fatimah scoffed. “Of course. You think I don’t know you? I knew you’d return to your usual bad habits.”

Maya opened the box, revealing home-cooked rice and vegetables. Warm, comforting, and filled with care. She felt a lump in her throat.

"Thank you, Fatimah."

Fatimah smiled. "I told you. You may be all alone, but I won't let you destroy yourself."

Maya looked down, feeling a mix of gratitude and guilt. Fatimah had a family, children to take care of, yet she still made time to look after Maya during office hours. But the loneliness returned at night. That evening, as she lay on her couch, Maya dialed Aaryan's number.

He picked up almost immediately. "Maya?"

"I collapsed at work," she said bluntly.

Aaryan sat up straight. "What? When?"

"Last week. I'm fine now."

"Maya," Aaryan's voice was filled with frustration. "This is exactly what I kept telling you! You're pushing yourself too hard."

Maya exhaled. "I know."

"You're still having headaches, aren't you?"

Maya hesitated. "Yeah."

There was silence for a moment before Aaryan spoke again. "You need to slow down, Maya. This isn't worth your health."

Maya closed her eyes. "I know, Aaryan. But I don't know how to stop."

Aaryan sighed. "Then let me help you. Let me come to Malaysia. Even I need a break—I've been wanting a vacation for a while now. My Malaysia trip is still pending, so why not now? I'll come for two weeks, and you can show me around. It'll be good for both of us."

Maya smiled faintly. "Not yet. Soon."

Aaryan said in frustration, "You always say that."

Maya chuckled. "Because I mean it."

Aaryan shook his head but didn't argue. "Just... take care of yourself, okay?"

Maya's smile softened. "I will."

As they ended the call, Maya sat in silence, staring at the city lights outside her window. She had built a life of success, but at what cost? Fatimah cared for her during the day, Aaryan worried for her at night—but in the end, she was still alone. And the worst part? She had no idea how to change that.

*****

Two days later, a dull beeping sound echoed in the silent hospital room. The dim light above cast a soft glow over Maya's pale face. Her eyes fluttered slightly, caught between the realms of unconsciousness and wakefulness. Fatimah sat beside her, clutching Maya's cold hand between her own warm palms. Her usually composed face bore lines of exhaustion, her hijab slightly disheveled, and her eyes carrying the weight of sleepless nights. Then, a small movement, Maya's fingers twitched.

Fatimah straightened, leaning forward, her heart pounding. "Maya?" she whispered, voice shaky but hopeful.

Maya's eyelids fluttered before slowly, ever so slowly, opening. The ceiling swam into focus, blurred at the edges. The sharp scent of antiseptic filled the air, accompanied by the steady beeping of a monitor in the background.

Her vision was hazy at first, but then she saw her—Fatimah, sitting beside her, eyes filled with something unrecognizable. Relief? Pain? Something else?

"Where... am I?" Maya's voice came out hoarse, barely audible.

Fatimah tightened her grip on Maya's hand. "You're in the hospital."

Maya frowned; her mind was sluggish as she struggled to grasp her last memory. She had been in the office. A sharp pain had pierced her head. Dizziness. Then—darkness.

She looked at Fatimah, trying to read her expression, but something was off. The warmth in her friend's eyes was laced with something grim, something unsettling.

"How long have I been here?" Maya asked, her voice stronger this time.

Fatimah hesitated.

Maya noticed. "Fatimah," she pressed.

Fatimah swallowed hard. "You lost consciousness, Maya. For a day."

Maya blinked. "A day?"

Fatimah nodded. "You collapsed. The doctors kept you under observation, ran tests, stabilized you. They wanted to be sure you were okay before waking you."

Maya exhaled slowly, trying to process it. Twenty-four hours. Gone, just like that.

Before she could say anything else, the door opened. A doctor entered, flipping through her medical chart. His face was unreadable, but Maya sensed the tension in the room.

"Miss Maya," the doctor greeted, offering a polite smile. "I'm glad to see you awake."

Maya barely acknowledged him, still grappling with the revelation. "What happened to me?" she asked, eyes locking onto his.

The doctor glanced at Fatimah, who gave him a subtle nod. He sighed, pulled a chair close, and sat down. "Maya, I need you to listen carefully."

Maya swallowed. "Go on."

The doctor hesitated for a brief moment, then exhaled. "We ran several tests while you were unconscious."

Maya's hands clenched the bed sheet. "And?"

The doctor met her gaze. "You have a tumor, Maya."

The room fell silent.

Maya blinked, her mind momentarily blank. "A... tumor?"

The doctor nodded. "A malignant tumor. It's in an advanced stage."

The air in the room turned heavy.

Maya felt her chest tighten. "What does that mean?"

Fatimah's fingers trembled around Maya's hand, but she stayed silent.

The doctor's voice was calm yet firm. "Maya, it means you have brain cancer."

The words struck like a hammer.

A ringing filled her ears. Her vision swam. Brain cancer. No. That couldn't be right. She had headaches, sure. She was exhausted. But cancer?

She forced herself to speak, her voice barely above a whisper. "How... bad is it?"

The doctor's expression didn't change, but his words were like ice. "At this stage, it's incurable."

Maya's breath caught.

Fatimah's grip tightened, her own tears threatening to fall.

Maya licked her dry lips. "How long?"

The doctor hesitated. "Six months. Maybe five."

The air left Maya's lungs. Five months? That was it?

She let out a small, humorless laugh. "You're saying I have less than half a year to live?"

The doctor's silence was her answer.

Maya closed her eyes. Her heartbeat pounded in her ears. *Six months.*

Her mind spiraled, racing through everything she hadn't achieved. She had spent years chasing success, building a career, always looking ahead—but now, there was no future to chase. A bitter thought settled in her chest. She had always dreamed of traveling through Malaysia, exploring every hidden corner of her homeland, feeling the pulse of the country beyond the walls of an office. It had been her biggest dream. But would she ever get the chance now?

Thoughts from every corner of her mind flooded in—unfinished goals, unspoken words, unfulfilled promises. Time had always seemed endless. Now, it was slipping through her fingers like sand.

She had worked all her life, chased success, sacrificed everything—only to be given six months? It felt like a cruel joke.

Fatimah finally spoke, her voice breaking. "There's treatment, Maya. It won't cure it, but it could give you a couple more years—possibly."

Maya opened her eyes and turned to her friend. "Years? And what would those years look like? Stuck in hospitals? Endless treatments?"

Fatimah's lips trembled, but she didn't deny it.

Maya inhaled sharply, looking at the ceiling. "I don't know what to say."

The doctor nodded. "You don't have to decide now. Take your time. But don't wait too long."

Maya nodded absently. Her mind felt like it was floating, detached from reality.

The doctor stood up. "I'll give you some space." He glanced at Fatimah, then left the room.

The silence stretched between them.

Fatimah finally spoke, her voice barely holding together. "Maya..."

Maya turned to her, eyes strangely dry. "You knew, didn't you? Before I woke up."

Fatimah nodded, tears slipping down her face.

Maya gave a small smile, void of warmth. "That's why you looked at me like that."

Fatimah sniffled. "I wanted to tell you. But the doctor said..."

Maya shook her head. "It doesn't matter now."

After a long pause, Maya frowned. "Aaryan."

Fatimah stiffened.

Maya looked at her sharply. "He must've called. He must be worried."

Fatimah sighed. "He called—many times. I told him yesterday that you were hospitalized, and he was extremely worried."

Maya's heart ached. "Did you tell him?"

Fatimah hesitated. Then, slowly, she shook her head. "No."

Maya stared. "Why?"

Fatimah's voice was firm yet painful. "Because I knew he'd drop everything and come running here. And I didn't want him to see you like this before you knew the truth yourself."

Maya looked away, a storm of emotions raging inside her. She wanted to be angry—but she couldn't. Because Fatimah was right. She wasn't ready for Aaryan to know. Not yet.

She turned back to Fatimah, shaking. "But he will know."

Fatimah nodded. "Yes. But when you decide."

Maya leaned back against the pillow, staring at the ceiling.

Six months.

What was she going to do with six months? For the first time in her life, Maya had no plan—no escape, no ideas, nothing.

*****

The hospital room was quiet except for the rhythmic ticking of the wall clock and the occasional beep of the monitors beside Maya's bed. The dim glow of the bedside lamp cast long shadows on the pale blue walls, creating a scary stillness around her. Maya lay in bed, staring at the ceiling, her mind in turmoil. Sleep was out of the question. How could she sleep when her entire world had just collapsed?

The doctor's words echoed in her mind.

"Six months. Maybe five."

A tremor ran through her fingers as she gripped the side of the bed, the weight of those words settling heavily on her chest. Five months. That was all she had left.

A bitter laugh escaped her lips. "All these years... for what?" she whispered to herself.

Her life flashed before her eyes—not in a dramatic, cinematic way, but in a series of regrets, of things left undone, of roads never taken.

She thought about Aaryan.

"Maya, life is not just about earning. You need to live too."

How many times had he told her that? How many times had she shrugged it off with a laugh, telling him, *"Later. I'll enjoy later."*

But later never came.

Aaryan had always been balanced, knowing when to work and when to live. But Maya? She had been obsessed. Obsessed with achieving more, earning more, proving herself. And for what? She had cut off so many friends in the process. Her thoughts drifted back to college, to the endless nights spent with books and assignments, while others made memories. She had topped the exams, secured the best job, but what else had she gained?

Nothing.

Not friendships. Not experiences. Not life.

And her parents...

A sharp pain sliced through her chest as she thought about them. The parents she had lost. The ones she had barely had time to grieve. She had drowned herself in work after their deaths, believing that success would somehow fill the void.

But it never had.

Tears welled up in her eyes.

"I wasted it," she murmured, her voice cracking. "I wasted everything."

The night stretched on, silent and merciless. Maya lay in bed, her body motionless but her mind racing, revisiting every moment she had thrown away in her pursuit of success.

She had never traveled.

Never taken a break.

Never truly *lived.*

She wept—not for the future, but for the past. For life she had never allowed herself to have.

Time passed. The darkness outside the window remained unchanging. And then, somewhere in the depths of her despair, a new thought emerged.

"I still have time."

Not much. But enough.

She sat up slowly, wiping her tear-streaked face. Her heart still ached, but now there was something else—a faint ember of determination. She couldn't change the past. But she still had four or five months.

She could still *live.*

A slow breath filled her lungs as she steadied herself. The pain was still there, but now, it was accompanied by resolve. She would do everything she never did.

She would *travel.*

She would reconnect with old friends. She would live every moment as if it were her last—because, in reality, it was.

The night felt different now. The silence wasn't suffocating anymore. It was peaceful. She turned her head toward the window, waiting. For the first time in years, she was waiting for the sunrise. And when the first rays of light painted the sky in hues of gold and orange, she picked up her phone.

It was time to call Aaryan.

*****

The morning sunlight streamed through the hospital window, casting warm golden rays across the sterile white sheets of Maya's bed. The soft buzz of the city outside filtered into the quiet room, blending with the rhythmic beep of the heart monitor beside her. But today, Maya felt different. She was no longer drowning in despair.

She had made her decision. There was no point in fighting a battle she had already lost. She had spent too much time chasing a future that no longer existed. Now, she had a chance to do what she had always wanted—to live.

Maya pressed the nurse call button, and within moments, a young nurse stepped inside. "You called, Miss Tan?"

"Yes," Maya said with a radiant smile. "I'd like to speak to the doctor."

The nurse hesitated for a second, surprised by Maya's upbeat tone, before nodding. "Of course. I'll inform him right away."

A few minutes later, Dr. Li, the middle-aged oncologist with a kind face, walked in with his clipboard. He adjusted his glasses as he took a seat beside her bed. "Good morning, Maya. You seem... well, different today."

"I feel different, Doctor," Maya said, sitting up straighter. "I've thought a lot about this, and I've made up my mind. I don't want the treatment."

Dr. Li's expression turned serious. "Maya, I understand your feelings, but treatment could give you a couple more years"

"I don't want to spend my remaining time hooked up to machines, weak and sick," she interrupted gently. "I want to travel, to experience life before it's too late. I know the risks, and I'm ready to face them."

The doctor exhaled heavily. He had seen patients make this decision before, but it never got easier. "Are you absolutely sure?"

"Yes," she said firmly. "I've spent my whole life preparing for a future that's never going to come. I don't want to spend my last months the same way."

Dr. Li studied her face for a long moment before nodding. "Alright. I won't force you. But I'll prescribe strong painkillers and emergency medications. You'll need them when the symptoms worsen."

Maya nodded, relieved. "How soon can I be discharged?"

"In a week," he said. "We need to monitor you a little longer, just to make sure you're stable before leaving."

"That's perfect," she said, a genuine smile spreading across her face.

Dr. Li stood up, still visibly surprised but supportive. "I'll make the arrangements. If you ever change your mind, you know where to find me."

As soon as he left, Maya reached for her phone with trembling hands. There was only one person she needed to talk to right now.

Aaryan.

She dialed his number, and within seconds, he picked up. “Maya?” His voice was groggy, he must have been sleeping.

“Aaryan...” Her voice broke, and for a moment, she couldn’t speak.

Aaryan sat up straight, his heart pounding. “What’s wrong, Maya? Talk to me. I’ve been calling you for two days, but you haven’t responded. Fatimah told me you were hospitalized. I’m worried.”

She took a deep breath. “Aaryan... I’m dying.”

A heavy silence hung on the other end.

She continued, tears brimming in her eyes. “I have brain cancer. The doctors say I have five months at most.”

A sharp inhale. Then silence.

For a moment, there was no response, only the faint sound of his unsteady breathing. She could picture him—sitting up, running a hand through his hair, struggling to make sense of what he had just heard.

“Aaryan?” she whispered.

She heard his breath tremble. When he finally spoke, his voice was raw, shaken. “No... no, that’s not possible,” he whispered. “You were fine. You were... how can this be?”

Tears spilled onto Maya’s cheeks. “I don’t know. But it’s real.”

Aaryan struggled to find words, but all that came out was a choked sob. “Maya...”

For the first time, they both cried together over the phone, their silent sobs filling the space between them.

And then, in a voice heavy with determination, Aaryan said, "*I'm coming to Malaysia.*"

Aaryan's bond with Maya had been built over years—through endless conversations during college days, late-night debates about life, love, and the universe, and phone calls every other day even after they had moved to different countries. There were friendships that existed within the boundaries of time and place, and then there were friendships like theirs—ones that defied all logic, all distance. Aaryan didn't think twice about leaving everything behind for her, because some people become so deeply ingrained in you that no circumstance can ever erase them. And for Maya, in this cruel twist of fate, all she wanted was for him to be by her side—at least once, before time ran out. Friendships like theirs could cross all limits, unshaken even in the face of death.

This time, Maya didn't protest. She didn't tell him she was too busy. She didn't make excuses.

Instead, she whispered, "I can't wait."

Over the next few days, Maya remained in the hospital, but her mind was elsewhere. She was planning her dream journey. A long bucket list was forming in her journal—places she wanted to visit, things she wanted to do, foods she wanted to try.

Fatimah visited every other evening after work and called every day, her voice always filled with warmth. She supported Maya's decision to forgo treatment and make the most of the time she had left.

Meanwhile, on the other side of the world, Aaryan was a mess. His flight was booked. He would arrive in

Malaysia on Saturday evening. But he was restless. He spent hours on the internet, scouring medical journals, alternative treatments, clinical trials—anything that could save Maya. Each time he came up empty, his heart clenched tighter.

No cure. No hope. All he could do was be there for her.

The day Maya's discharge arrived, Fatimah was there, waiting with a soft smile and moist eyes. "Ready to go?"

Before discharging her, the hospital handed Maya a long diet chart along with a bundle of medicines and multivitamins to keep her going.

Maya grinned, despite her weakened body. "More than ever."

As they drove to Maya's apartment, the reality of her decision set in. She was leaving the life she had built—the corporate world, the endless work, the stress.

And she felt *free*.

Fatimah helped her settle in, making sure she had everything she needed before leaving for the night. "Call me if you need anything, okay?"

"I will."

As soon as she was alone, Maya rushed to her journal. She flipped through the pages, finalizing her itinerary. She had only months left, and there was no time to waste. The Malaccan streets, Langkawi's beaches, The Cameron Highlands, Penang's food. And of course, Aaryan's grand tour of Malaysia.

The thought made her giddy with excitement. She checked the time—just one more day. Aaryan would land in Malaysia tomorrow evening. That night, she lay in bed, staring outside the window. She had spent her whole life waiting for the perfect moment to live. Now, she was finally doing it. And this time, it wasn't just a dream.

Her *last wish* was about to come true, a wish she had thought of before, but now, it was her last.

*****

The airport was bustling with activity. Travelers hurried past with luggage carts, families reunited with laughter and tears, and the air smelled of coffee and distant perfume. But Aaryan stood still, his backpack slung over one shoulder, his eyes scanning the arrival hall. His heart was heavy, burdened with the cruel reality that had brought him here. He had been waiting for this trip for years—but not like this. Not under these circumstances.

As he exhaled a deep breath, trying to steady his emotions, he suddenly felt two warm arms wrap around him from behind, squeezing him so tight that for a moment, all the sadness he carried was replaced by something else—pure, overwhelming love.

"Aaryan!" Maya screamed in his back, her voice filled with joy, relief, and a hint of something deeper gratitude. "Thank you for coming!"

Aaryan's body tensed in shock, but within seconds, his hands reached for hers, pulling them forward. Then, turning around swiftly, he pulled her into an even tighter hug, wrapping his arms around her as though he would never let go.

Maya buried her face in his chest, and Aaryan closed his eyes, inhaling the familiar scent of her. He gently pulled her back just a little, enough to cup her face in his hands. He lifted her chin, his thumbs brushing against her cheeks as he studied her face—she was smiling, but there was exhaustion beneath it. There was pain she was trying to hide.

He leaned forward and pressed a lingering kiss on her forehead, his lips trembling as they met her skin. Maya smiled, holding his arms. Then, once again, she hugged him—tightly, desperately, as though trying to tell him everything she couldn't say in words. For the next few minutes, they simply stood there, in the middle of the airport, hugging each other in silence. Nothing else mattered at that moment. Maya pulled Aaryan's luggage and led him towards the parking lot, her energy still strangely high.

"You're driving?" Aaryan asked, eyeing her suspiciously.

"Of course!" she said, grinning. "I'm not dying today, relax!"

Aaryan's heart clenched at the way she casually joked about it.

As they settled into the car, Aaryan fastened his seatbelt, still watching her carefully. She was unusually... happy. Excited, even. It felt surreal, like a contradiction to everything she had told him over the phone. The car moved smoothly towards Kuala Lumpur, neon lights reflecting off the windshield. For a long time, Aaryan stayed quiet, staring at her as she hummed along with the radio.

"You look happy," he finally said.

Maya glanced at him and smiled. "I am."

Aaryan swallowed hard. "Maya... I don't understand how."

Maya sighed, her grip on the steering wheel tightening just slightly. "I had two choices, Aaryan. I could either spend my last months crying and regretting my life, or I could live the life I never got to live. And I choose to live."

Aaryan exhaled, running a hand through his hair. "You're incredible, you know that?"

Maya smirked. "I know."

He chuckled softly, but the laughter didn't quite reach his eyes. He was still in shock.

The drive took about fifty minutes, and when they reached Maya's apartment, Aaryan stepped inside, taking a quick look around. It was neat, minimalistic, but it didn't feel like a home. It felt... temporary.

Maya disappeared into the kitchen and returned with a cold mug of coffee, handing it to him.

"Here," she said, sitting across from him.

Aaryan took a sip, nodding in approval. "This is good." Maya smiled but didn't respond. Instead, she placed her hands on the table, folding her fingers together. For a moment, there was silence.

Then, softly, Maya said, "I have four to five months left."

The words hung in the air, suffocating, pressing against Aaryan's chest like a weight too heavy to carry. His grip on the mug tightened, his eyes stinging as he looked at her. And just like that, his tears spilled. Maya followed immediately, her tears falling freely. They didn't say anything. There was nothing to say. They just sat there, crying, mourning something that hadn't even happened yet.

When the sobs quieted, Aaryan wiped his face with his sleeve and looked at Maya seriously.

"You still have time," he said. "We can try treatment. We can"

"No, Aaryan," Maya interrupted firmly. "I've made my decision."

"But"

"No," she said again. "I will not spend my last days in a hospital bed, weak and helpless. I don't want to die surrounded by machines."

Aaryan clenched his jaw, swallowing down another wave of emotion. After a long pause, he finally sighed, reaching forward and pulling her into another hug.

"Alright," he murmured. "I won't lecture you. We'll do this your way."

Maya smiled against his shoulder. "You know, you never really had a choice."

Aaryan chuckled, shaking his head. "You never listen to anyone anyway."

That was the first time they both laughed that night.

Aaryan leaned back in his chair, stretching his arms. "I'm starving, by the way. That flight was torture."

Maya gasped. "Oh my god! I totally forgot. Let's eat out!"

Aaryan raised an eyebrow. "You don't cook at home?"

Maya grinned mischievously. "Not anymore. And from today, I will never cook again!"

Aaryan laughed. "What? Why?"

"Because," she said, standing up dramatically, "I'm going to eat every dish in Malaysia before I die!"

Aaryan's laughter faded slightly at the last part of her sentence, but he forced himself to smile.

"You think four to five months is enough for all that?" he asked playfully.

Maya pretended to look thoughtful. "Honestly? No. Malaysia has too much good food. I might have to extend my death date."

Aaryan burst out laughing. "You're ridiculous."

"And you love me for it," Maya said with a wink.

Aaryan's smile softened. "Yeah. I do."

Maya put on her sandals, and Aaryan followed her out of the apartment. As they stepped into the bustling streets of Kuala Lumpur, Maya spread her arms wide, inhaling deeply.

"This," she said, looking up at the stars, "is the start of my greatest adventure."

Aaryan watched her, his heart aching and full at the same time. He didn't know how he was going to survive watching her go through this. But he knew one thing for sure, he was going to make sure she lived the happiest months of her life. And so, with that silent promise, he took her hand, and together, they walked into the night, ready to chase her dreams.

*****

The last week had been a whirlwind of decisions, emotions, and irreversible changes. Maya, in her usual determined fashion, had wasted no time. She had divided her wealth, keeping just enough for her remaining days, and pledged the rest to a cancer charity for children. The thought of young lives fighting the same fate she was facing broke her heart, and she wanted to leave something behind—something meaningful.

But while Maya was preparing for the end, Aaryan was preparing for something else entirely. He had made up his mind. He was going to stay with Maya. Not just for a few days, not just for a trip—he was going to be by her side until the very end. To do that, he had done something drastic—he had resigned from his job. Because more than anything, he wanted to be there for his best friend, taking care of her until she passed away. The decision wasn't easy, but it wasn't difficult either. The only hard part was telling his parents.

Although Aaryan had already told his parents about Maya's death before departing for Kuala Lumpur, he had lied and said he would be back in a week after meeting her. But now, as he sat on the balcony of Maya's apartment, overlooking the Kuala Lumpur skyline, he knew he couldn't keep up the lie for long. Taking a deep breath, he dialed his father's number.

The phone rang twice before his father picked up.

"Aaryan? Beta, how are you?" his father asked, his voice warm with affection. In India, 'beta' is a common way for a father to address his son—a word filled with love and care. But Aaryan knew that warmth would soon fade.

He took another deep breath. "Papa... I need to talk to you and Maa. Is she there?"

"Yes, hold on."

A few seconds later, his mother's voice chimed in. "Aaryan, is everything okay? You sound serious."

Aaryan clenched his jaw, trying to steady himself. "Maa, Papa, I've made a decision. I have resigned from my job."

After a few seconds of silence, "WHAT?" His father's voice boomed through the speaker. "What nonsense are you saying? Why would you do something like that?"

Aaryan exhaled, closing his eyes. "Because I need to be here. With Maya."

Another silence. This one heavier, colder.

His mother spoke next, her voice trembling. "Aaryan... tell me this isn't what I think it is. Tell me you haven't thrown away everything for..." She hesitated. "For a girl who is..."

Aaryan cut her off. "For a girl who is dying, Maa? Yes. That's exactly what I've done."

His mother gasped, and his father let out a bitter laugh. "Aaryan, do you even hear yourself? You left your job, your career, your future, for a girl who won't even be here in a few months? Have you lost your mind?"

Aaryan's grip on the phone tightened. "No, Papa. For the first time in my life, I think I've found it."

His father scoffed. "This is madness. This is stupid. We didn't send you to the best schools, didn't raise you with values, just so you could throw away your life over emotions!"

Aaryan's eyes burned, but he refused to back down. "You're wrong, Papa. You raised me with values. You raised me to be a good person, a loyal person. And what kind of man would I be if I abandoned my best friend when she needed me the most?"

His mother sniffled on the other end. "Beta... we understand that you care for her. But you have to think about your own future. What will happen to you after Maya is gone?"

Aaryan looked up at the sky, blinking rapidly. "Maa... Maya is not just someone I care about. She's, my family. And right now, she doesn't have anyone else. She spent her whole life chasing success, thinking she had time for everything else later. But now, she doesn't. And I won't let her live these last few months alone. I won't let her die alone."

His father's voice was sharp. "You are being emotional, Aaryan. You are ruining your life for nothing."

Aaryan's chest heaved. "For nothing?!" His voice cracked. "Maya is not nothing! Our friendship is not nothing! Maybe you don't understand this, Papa, but I do. Some things in life are more important than careers, more important than stability, more important than logic. Maya is my best friend. And I will stand by her, no matter what it costs me."

His father's breathing was heavy through the phone. "And after she's gone? What then?"

Aaryan's throat tightened. He had asked himself the same question countless times. But he already knew the answer.

"Then, I will live with no regrets."

A long, unbearable silence.

Then his mother whispered, "Aaryan... will this make you happy?"

Aaryan's voice softened. "Maa, it's not about my happiness. It's about Maya's. And if I can give her that, then yes... that will make me happy."

His mother sobbed quietly.

His father let out a deep sigh, defeated. "You've already decided."

Aaryan nodded. "Yes, Papa, I have."

"Then do what you must. But don't expect us to support this decision."

A lump formed in Aaryan's throat. "I don't expect anything, Papa. I just wanted you to know why I'm doing this."

His father didn't respond. The call ended with a click. Aaryan closed his eyes, breathing deeply. He had done what he had to do, and he had no regrets. Once the call ended, Aaryan stepped into the living area and found Maya on the floor, scribbling furiously in a notebook. Her excitement was evident, her eyes glowing with a light he hadn't seen in years.

She looked up at him. "You spent a lot of time on the balcony. Everything okay?"

Aaryan forced a smile and walked over, sitting beside her. He looked at the notebook in her lap. "What's this?"

Maya grinned. "Our itinerary."

Aaryan chuckled. "You made an itinerary?"

Maya smirked. "Of course. You think I'll just sit back and let the days pass? Nope. We have things to do, places to go, foods to eat. We are going to live, Aaryan."

Aaryan watched her, his chest filling with a mix of sorrow and admiration. She had every reason to crumble, yet here she was, planning her last adventure with more enthusiasm than most people planned their entire lives.

He reached out, taking her hand. "Then let's live, Maya."

She pinched his hand, smiling. "Yes. Let's live."

And just like that, their journey began. Aaryan had fought for this moment, and he would make sure every second counted.

*****

Aaryan lay on the bed in the guest room of Maya's apartment, staring at the ceiling. He had tossed and turned for hours, but sleep evaded him. His mind was too restless, too full. The past few days had been overwhelming, quitting his job, standing up to his parents, traveling to Malaysia, and then seeing Maya like this. She was glowing with excitement, but beneath that radiance, he could see the exhaustion, the weight of what was to come. He exhaled heavily, knowing that sleep wouldn't come anytime soon. He needed air. Slipping out of bed, he walked towards the balcony, expecting to be alone. But as he stepped outside, he saw her.

Maya stood at the edge of the railing, gazing at the stars. A soft breeze lifted her hair, and the faint glow of the city lights reflected in her eyes. She was lost in thought, completely still, as if absorbing every bit of the night sky.

Aaryan hesitated for a moment before speaking. "Oh... hi, Maya. Can't sleep?"

Maya didn't answer immediately. Instead, she turned her head slightly, a soft smile on her lips.

"Do you need coffee?" she asked.

Aaryan chuckled. "You're offering coffee at three in the morning?"

Maya shrugged. "Why not? If we can't sleep, we might as well enjoy something good."

Aaryan nodded. "Then yes, I'd love a cup."

Maya disappeared into the kitchen while Aaryan leaned against the balcony railing, looking at the skyline of Kuala Lumpur. The Petronas Towers stood tall in the distance, their lights shimmering like diamonds in the dark. A few minutes later, Maya returned with two steaming mugs. She handed one to Aaryan before taking a sip from her own. They stood in silence for a moment, sipping their coffee, breathing in the night air.

Finally, Aaryan spoke. "So, tell me about the plans."

Maya turned to him, raising an eyebrow. "Plans?"

Aaryan smiled. "Yes, the grand travel plans. You said you had an itinerary, right?"

Maya chuckled. "I do. And it's packed with everything I always wanted to do."

Aaryan sipped his coffee. "I'm listening."

Maya set her mug down on the balcony ledge and stretched her arms.

"First, we'll start with Langkawi. The beaches there are unreal—white sand, turquoise water, and the most breathtaking sunsets you can imagine."

Aaryan nodded, intrigued. "Sounds great. What's next?"

Maya's eyes twinkled. "Then we'll head to Penang. The street food there is legendary, and the old town is full of history. You'll love exploring the murals and the little cafés hidden in the alleys."

Aaryan grinned. "Food and history? Sounds like a perfect mix. What else?"

Maya took another sip of coffee, her expression turning softer. "Then, we'll go to the Cameron Highlands.

The tea plantations there are stunning. I always wanted to sit on a hill, sip fresh tea, and just... exist."

Aaryan watched her carefully. "And after that?"

Maya hesitated before speaking. "Then we go to Malacca. It's my favorite place, so we'll spend a lot of days there. The heritage, the riverwalk, the night market—I could lose myself in that city forever."

Aaryan smiled. "You've really thought of everything, haven't you?"

Maya nodded, looking at the sky again. "I have to. I don't have time to waste anymore."

Aaryan's smile faded slightly, but he quickly masked it. He didn't want to bring the mood down. Instead, he clinked his mug against hers. "Then let's make it happen."

Maya looked at him, her expression unreadable. Then, slowly, she smiled. "Yes. Let's."

The night stretched on, and they kept talking—about places, about food, about their old college days. They laughed over memories of exams, of how Maya would always be buried in books while Aaryan would convince her to take breaks.

Maya sipped the last of her coffee and sighed. "You know, Aaryan... I've been thinking a lot."

Aaryan turned to her. "About what?"

Maya hesitated before speaking. "About life. About how much I focused on things that don't really matter. I thought success meant working hard, earning big, being at the top. But what does that mean now? Now that I have months left... what does any of it mean?"

Aaryan remained silent.

Maya turned to him, her eyes serious. "I wasted so much time, Aaryan. So much. And I can't get it back."

Aaryan groaned. "Maya... you did what you thought was right at the time. You can't blame yourself."

Maya smiled sadly. "Maybe. But that's why these next months are so important to me. I won't waste another second."

Aaryan reached out and embraced her hand. "Then we won't. We'll make every moment count."

Maya held onto his hand for a moment before pulling away and stretching. "Okay, enough serious talk. Let's focus on what's ahead. Tomorrow, we start exploring."

Aaryan was excited. "I can't wait."

Maya smiled mischievously and said, "Oh, you'll love it. There will be such a huge variety—Malay, Chinese, and local delicacies—that you'll forget all about your Indian food."

Aryan shook his head firmly. "No way! Indian food is the best in the world. I don't think Malaysian food even comes close."

Maya laughed. "Is that a challenge?"

"Call it whatever you want," Aryan smirked. "But I doubt anything can beat a plate of butter chicken and naan."

"Just wait until you try our nasi lemak and char kway teow," she teased. "You might just change your mind."

It was almost 3 AM, and they both started feeling tired. Aryan let out a yawn, while Maya stretched her arms, her eyelids growing heavy.

Maya yawned and said, "Okay, okay. That's enough. We need some sleep if we want to survive our adventure tomorrow."

Aaryan nodded. "Agreed. Let's get some rest."

As they walked back inside, Maya turned to him and smirked. "And Aaryan?"

"Yeah?"

"Be ready. Because tomorrow, we begin the greatest trip of our lives."

Aaryan smiled. "I wouldn't have it any other way."

And with that, the night slowly faded, giving way to the first hints of dawn. In just two hours, the sun would rise, but for now, the world remained quiet, wrapped in the lingering stillness of the night.

*****

The soft glow of dawn crept into the room, casting a golden hue over the walls. The world outside was slowly waking up, but Maya had already been awake. Excitement coursed through her veins, and sleep was the last thing on her mind. Today was the day—the day her journey would truly begin.

She had spent the past few days planning, making lists, checking and rechecking every detail of their upcoming trip. The only thing left to do now was to wake up the person who would be her travel companion for the next few days, Aaryan. A mischievous grin spread across her face as she tiptoed into his room. He lay sprawled on the bed, his face half-buried in the pillow, breathing steadily. His exhaustion from the flight two days ago was evident.

"Wake up, sleepyhead!" she called out cheerfully, but he didn't stir.

She tried again, this time yanking the blanket off him in one swift motion. Aaryan groaned, curling into a ball.

"Maya... what the hell? Let me sleep for ten more minutes," he mumbled groggily.

Maya rolled her eyes. "Nope. Not happening. We're hitting the road early, and you don't get to be lazy."

She grabbed his arm and started pulling him up. Aaryan resisted, his body limp like a rag doll.

"Maya, have some mercy! It's too early for this energy!" he protested.

Maya uttered, "Oh, don't be dramatic. You'll thank me when we're having an amazing breakfast in Ipoh."

At the mention of food, Aaryan finally opened one eye. "Ipoh? What's so special about breakfast there?"

Maya said, "You'll find out soon enough. Now get up and freshen up. We leave in thirty minutes."

Defeated, Aaryan groaned again but dragged himself out of bed. As he trudged to the bathroom, Maya returned to the living room, where their packed bags were lined up neatly near the door. Everything was set. By the time Aaryan returned, looking fresher but still slightly drowsy, Maya handed him a steaming cup of coffee.

"Here. This will help," she said.

Aaryan took a sip, sighed in satisfaction, and nodded. "Okay. Now I'm awake."

Maya clapped her hands. "Great! Let's go."

With that, they stepped out, loaded their bags into the car, and started their journey.

As soon as they hit the highway, Aaryan's grogginess melted away, replaced by awe.

"Wow," he murmured, his eyes widening as he took in the surroundings.

Maya chuckled. "What?"

Aaryan gestured outside. "The roads, the greenery, the cleanliness—everything looks so... perfect."

Maya smiled knowingly. "Malaysia takes pride in its infrastructure. And see those trees? Those are palm trees. We have a lot of palm oil plantations here."

Aaryan nodded, still in awe. "It's so different from back home. And people actually follow traffic rules here!

No unnecessary honking, no reckless overtaking. In India, indicators are just decorative lights."

Maya laughed. "You're not wrong. The driving culture here is way more disciplined."

Aaryan leaned back in his seat, taking it all in. "I have to admit, I didn't expect to be this impressed. But I am."

Maya smirked. "This is just the beginning. Wait till you see what's ahead."

She pressed down on the accelerator slightly, the car gliding smoothly along the highway.

"So, where's our first stop?" Aaryan asked.

"Ipoh. We won't be staying too long, just stopping for breakfast. I know the perfect place."

Aaryan raised an eyebrow. "And what exactly are we eating?"

Maya's face lit up. "Curry mee, dim sum, and Ipoh white coffee. Do you know dim sum?"

Aaryan scoffed. "Of course! They're super popular in North India. I love them. But I've never heard of curry mee."

Maya beamed. "It's a coconut-based curry broth with noodles. You can add different toppings, but I like mine with tofu."

Aaryan's mouth watered at the description. "That sounds incredible!"

Maya nodded. "It is. Just wait till you taste it."

The anticipation of good food made the rest of the drive fly by. Within two hours, they reached the charming town of Ipoh. Maya pulled up in front of a bustling eatery, the air filled with the aroma of spices and freshly brewed coffee.

"This place," she declared, "serves the best breakfast in town."

Aaryan glanced around, taking in the old-school charm of the café. "Alright, I'm intrigued. Let's do this."

They found a table, and Maya placed the order. Within minutes, steaming bowls of curry mee, delicate dim sum, and cups of frothy white coffee arrived.

Aaryan took a cautious sip of the coffee first. His eyes bulged. "This is so smooth. I've never had coffee like this before!"

Maya said proudly, "That's because it's made differently. The beans are roasted with margarine, which gives them a unique caramelized taste."

Next, Aaryan picked up his chopsticks and took a bite of the curry mee. His expression changed instantly.

"Oh my God. This is amazing!" he exclaimed.

Maya laughed. "Told you!"

He eagerly moved on to the dim sum, savoring each bite.

"Maya, I think I'm in love with this food," he declared dramatically.

Maya smirked. "Good. Because we have a lot more to try on this trip."

They ate in comfortable silence, enjoying every bite. When they were done, Aaryan leaned back, patting his stomach.

"That was perfect. I don't think I can eat another bite."

Maya chuckled. "Oh, just wait till lunch. You'll change your mind."

Aaryan groaned. "You're going to make me fat."

Maya shrugged. "Life's too short to count calories, my friend."

Aaryan's smile faded slightly. He knew she was right but hearing it from her held a deeper meaning. For a moment, neither of them spoke. They just sat there, appreciating the moment.

Finally, Maya clapped her hands. "Alright! Time to get moving. We have a ferry to catch."

Aaryan nodded, shaking off his thoughts. "Let's do it."

Back in the car, they continued towards Kuala Kedah, where they would take the ferry to Langkawi.

Aaryan stared out at the road ahead. "You know, I have a feeling this trip is going to be the best journey of my life."

Maya glanced at him, smiling softly. "Mine too."

And with that, they drove on, the open road stretching ahead, leading them towards adventure, discovery, and memories they would cherish forever.

*****

The car hummed steadily along the well-paved highway as Maya adjusted the air-conditioning, ensuring the cool breeze swept over both of them. The Malaysian sun was bright and merciless, but inside the car, the atmosphere was filled with excitement, anticipation, and the lingering flavors of their delightful breakfast in Ipoh.

Aaryan, still soaking in the experiences of the day, turned to Maya and asked, "So, where are we heading next?"

Maya smiled, her fingers drumming on the steering wheel. "Next stop—Kuala Kedah Ferry Terminal. About three hours from here. From there, we'll take the ferry to Langkawi, and guess what? We're taking the car with us!"

Aaryan's eyes lit up with excitement. "Wait, what? We're putting the car on a ferry? I've never done that before!"

Maya chuckled. "Neither have I. But I booked it online. It usually takes about 90 minutes to reach Langkawi's Kuah Terminal. It's going to be an experience."

Aaryan leaned back, grinning. "That sounds amazing. I can't believe we're doing this. I mean, Langkawi—just the name sounds magical."

Maya nodded, her eyes shimmering with anticipation. "It's my dream destination. I've never been there either. I've only seen pictures and heard my friends talk about it. They say it's nothing short of a wonder."

She pressed the accelerator slightly, feeling a rush of adrenaline as they moved further along the highway. The smooth roads, the greenery lining both sides, and the occasional glimpse of traditional kampung houses on stilts made the journey picturesque.

Aaryan, who had been lost in thought, kept looking out the window. He had traveled extensively in India and other countries, but something about this place felt different.

"This is incredible," he muttered, almost to himself.

Maya smirked. "What is?"

Aaryan gestured outside. "Everything—the trees, the housing, the infrastructure. It's so well-maintained. I expected Malaysia to be nice, but I never imagined it to be this beautiful. I mean, I've always thought of it as just another Southeast Asian country, but man, I was so wrong."

Maya grinned. "I told you so! You never believed me."

Aaryan chuckled. "You did. And now I have to admit, I like it very much."

They continued driving, occasionally chatting about random things—music, childhood memories, their college days, and all the moments they had missed out on over the years. Maya felt a strange sense of comfort. She was finally living, truly living, not just working to earn another paycheck.

After about an hour, Aaryan suddenly adjusted in his seat. "Hey, can we stop somewhere? I need to use the loo."

Maya nodded. "Sure. There's an R&R (Rest & Recreation) stop nearby. We'll pull over there."

Maya exited the highway, following the signs for the nearest R&R station. As they approached, Aaryan's eyes widened. The place was enormous. Rows of shops, food stalls, petrol stations, and even prayer rooms were spread out in an organized manner. There was a dedicated parking area, and everything looked spotless.

"Whoa," Aaryan muttered. "This is not what I expected. I mean, we have *dhabas* (roadside restaurants) and small stops in India, but this is on another level. Is this the biggest one in Malaysia?"

Maya shook her head, smiling. "Nope. There are many like this along the highways. It's pretty common here."

Aaryan looked around, taking it all in. "This is impressive. The way everything is structured—it's like a small township."

They parked the car and headed toward the restroom. Once they were done, Aaryan wandered into a convenience store and picked up a few things—some soft drinks, chewing gum, and a pack of toffees.

"Not getting anything to eat?" Maya teased as she joined him at the counter.

Aaryan shook his head. "Still full of that insane breakfast. I swear, that curry mee and dim sum were a deadly combo."

Maya laughed. "Told you to pace yourself."

Once they were back on the road, Aaryan started making small comparisons between Malaysia and India. While he admitted that some things back home were equally impressive, he couldn't deny that Malaysia had an edge in terms of organization and infrastructure. Maya listened, amused. She knew he was slowly falling in love with the country.

After driving for about thirty minutes, Maya suddenly pulled over near a roadside stall. The bright yellow signboard displayed images of a spiky fruit, and the air around them carried a pungent, almost overpowering scent.

Aaryan frowned. "What's this place?"

Maya grinned mischievously. "This," she said, stepping out of the car, "is where you get to try something you won't find in India."

Curious, Aaryan followed her to the stall, eyeing the large, thorny fruits stacked on the wooden counter. "Looks like jackfruit," he remarked.

Maya shook her head, amused. "No, this is durian."

Aaryan raised an eyebrow. "Durian? I've never heard about it."

Turning to the stall owner, she spoke in Malay, requesting a Musang King variety and asking him to cut it open. Within moments, the vendor split the fruit, revealing its golden-yellow flesh. The sharp scent intensified, making Aaryan instinctively step back.

He covered his nose slightly. "Are you sure people eat this?"

Maya laughed. "You're about to find out."

She picked up a piece and, without giving him a chance to protest, held it up to his lips. "Come on, Aaryan. Just one bite."

Hesitant, he finally opened his mouth, and she gently placed the soft, creamy flesh on his tongue. The moment it touched his taste buds, an explosion of flavors hit him—sweet, salty, candy-like, with a strange gingery undertone. Aaryan's expression shifted as he tried to make sense of the unexpected medley of flavors.

Maya watched in amusement. "Well?"

Aaryan chewed slowly, still trying to decipher whether he liked it or not. He finally swallowed and exhaled, looking utterly bewildered. "I... I don't know what just happened."

Maya burst into laughter. "That's the durian experience for you!"

Aaryan stared at the remaining pieces. "It's not bad... but it's not exactly good either."

"Typical first-timer reaction," she teased. "Don't worry, it grows on you."

He wasn't so sure, but he had to admit—Malaysia never ceased to surprise him.

As they drove further, Aaryan's eyelids grew heavy. The rhythmic buzz of the car, combined with the gentle movement of the road, made it impossible for him to stay awake.

"I think I need a power nap," he murmured.

Maya glanced at him. "Go ahead. I'll wake you up when we reach."

Aaryan adjusted his seat and closed his eyes. Within minutes, he was fast asleep.

Maya, on the other hand, was wide awake. She switched on the music, scrolling through her playlist until she found her favorite singer—Datuk Seri Siti Nurhaliza.

The soft, melodious voice filled the car, and Maya hummed along. She had always admired Siti. There was a time when she dreamed of being a singer herself, but life had taken her in a different direction. She had an average vocal quality, nowhere near Siti's, but that never stopped her from singing along.

As the bright afternoon sun shone overhead, casting warm golden rays, Maya couldn't help but feel at peace. She was on the road, going to her dream destination, with her best friend beside her. For the first time in years, she felt truly happy.

After about 20 minutes, Maya glanced at Aaryan and smirked. She snapped her fingers in front of his face.

"Wake up, mister!"

Aaryan stirred, blinking rapidly. "Huh? Have we reached Langkawi?"

Maya rolled her eyes. "No, sleepyhead. We're at Kuala Kedah. Now we take the ferry to the 'Jewel of Kedah—Langkawi."

Aaryan stretched and looked around. They had pulled into a busy terminal, with multiple ferry services visible in the distance. There were long lines of cars waiting to be loaded onto the ferries.

He turned to Maya, excitement returning to his voice. "So, how does this work? We just drive onto the ferry?"

Maya nodded. "Exactly. We have a reserved spot. We drive up, park the car inside, and then we go up to the passenger deck."

Aaryan said excitedly, "This is going to be epic."

Maya couldn't agree more. The next leg of their journey was about to begin, and she was ready for the adventure that awaited them in Langkawi. With a deep breath, she drove towards the loading area, feeling a mix of excitement and anticipation. Langkawi—the dream she had long held in her heart—was finally within reach.

*****

The ferry glided smoothly over the shimmering waters of the Andaman Sea, carrying Aaryan and Maya toward their much-awaited destination—Langkawi, the Jewel of Kedah. Aaryan stood near the railing, feeling the salty wind brush against his face. He turned to Maya, who was leaning beside him, her hair dancing wildly in the sea breeze.

"Langkawi," Aaryan murmured, taking in the approaching island with its lush green hills and golden beaches. "It looks surreal."

Maya smiled. "I told you it would be beautiful. And we've only just begun."

The ferry docked at Kuah Terminal, and as soon as they drove off the ramp, the real adventure began. The roads of Langkawi stretched ahead, lined with coconut trees and glimpses of the ocean peeking through the spaces between them. The air smelled of salt, freedom, and a promise of new memories.

Maya navigated through the island roads skillfully until they reached their resort, a beautiful beachside retreat located on Pantai Tengah. As they pulled up, Aaryan noticed how the resort blended seamlessly with nature—wooden structures, palm-thatched roofs, and an open lobby that overlooked the endless blue sea.

The moment Maya parked the car, they flung the doors open, tossed their luggage onto the lobby floor, and without a second thought, sprinted toward the beach. The wind hit their faces, carrying the scent of the ocean, while the waves sang a soothing melody. Their feet sank into the warm golden sand as they ran without a destination, just pure, uninhibited joy. Like two carefree kids, they picked up sticks and began drawing random shapes in the sand. Aaryan wrote his name in bold letters, while Maya sketched a poorly shaped heart beside it.

"Is that supposed to be a heart?" Aaryan teased.

Maya scoffed. "It's abstract art. You wouldn't understand."

Laughing, they tossed away their sticks and ran toward the water, where the sea kissed the shore in soft, foamy waves. They stepped in ankle-deep water, feeling the coolness rush over their skin, and before long, they were splashing water at each other like mischievous kids.

Maya let out a loud, spontaneous laugh, the kind of laughter that didn't belong to someone who knew her time was slipping away. In that moment, she had forgotten everything—her illness, her fate, her fears. Right now, she was just Maya, a girl standing on the beach, living in the moment.

Aaryan, watching her, felt an unexplainable warmth in his heart. If he could capture one memory of Maya forever, it would be this—her laughter blending with the sound of the sea, her eyes sparkling brighter than the sunlit waves.

As the water swirled around their feet, Aaryan suddenly crouched down and began digging through the wet sand.

Maya tilted her head. "What are you doing?"

"Looking for seashells," Aaryan said, his voice full of childlike excitement. "This is my first time at a beach. I've only ever seen this on television."

Maya's expression softened. "Really?"

Aaryan nodded. "Yeah. I grew up in Delhi—no beaches, just roads and buildings. This... this is something else."

They both sank onto the soft sand, their fingers absentmindedly tracing patterns in the grains. The vast, endless sea stretched before them, its waves rolling in a steady rhythm, whispering secrets to the shore. The sun hung low in the sky, painting the horizon in shades of gold and crimson, its reflection shimmering on the water like scattered jewels. For a moment, neither of them spoke, simply soaking in the beauty around them.

After a moment of silence, Maya stood up and dusted the sand off her hands. "Come on, let's explore."

And so, they did.

They wandered across the shoreline, sometimes sitting on wooden shacks, sometimes running and jumping into the shallow waves. They took photos, preserving the warm glow of the sun as it dipped below the horizon behind them. For a while, time didn't exist. There was only them, the sea, and the boundless sky.

As the evening deepened, Aaryan checked his watch. "We should probably check in and rest a bit."

Maya nodded. "You go ahead. I'll be right behind you."

Aaryan jogged toward the lobby while Maya remained near the shore. With the wooden stick she had been playing with earlier, she knelt and slowly, carefully wrote in the sand:

"I want to live."

She stared at the words, her heart pounding. It was the first time she had admitted it—to herself, to the universe.

A wave crashed against the shore, washing over her words, erasing them as if they had never existed. Maya closed her eyes, exhaling. Perhaps it was a sign. With one last look at the sea, she turned and walked back toward Aaryan. The check-in process was quick. They received the keys to their respective rooms, two separate ones, because, of course, they were just friends. Neither of them had the energy to grab dinner. The exhaustion from the journey, the excitement of the day, and the comfort of their beds pulled them into deep sleep almost instantly. Before parting for the night, they made one final promise.

"Breakfast at eight," Aaryan said, yawning.

Maya grinned. "Don't be late."

The next morning, Aaryan arrived at the breakfast counter right on time. The dining area was an open deck, overlooking the sea. The scent of freshly brewed coffee mixed with the salty ocean breeze, creating an intoxicatingly relaxing atmosphere. Maya was already there, sitting by the edge, her eyes lost in the vastness of the water.

Aaryan slid into the chair beside her. "Deep thoughts?"

Maya turned to him with a little smile. "Just... appreciating the view."

For a while, they sat in silence, sipping their coffee, absorbing the serenity of the morning. Then Aaryan broke the silence.

"Where are we headed today?"

Maya smirked. "No plans. We'll just drive and stop wherever we feel like."

Aaryan raised an eyebrow. "That's a bold move for someone who usually plans everything."

Maya stretched her arms lazily. "Today, I just want to get lost in Langkawi."

Aaryan giggled. "Then let's get lost."

With that, their second day in Langkawi began—an adventure with no maps, no schedules, just the road ahead and the promise of discovering something beautiful together.

*****

The morning air in Langkawi carried a distinct scent—a mix of salty sea breeze, damp earth from the previous night's rain, and the distant aroma of local street food being prepared in the sleepy village corners. As Aaryan and Maya walked toward their car, parked just outside the resort, they felt an excitement bubbling within them.

"Ready for today's adventure?" Maya asked, tossing the car keys into the air and catching them effortlessly.

Aaryan said curiously, "Absolutely.

And with that, they began their journey, the island unfolding before them like a dream. Their first stop was Perdana Quay Lighthouse. As they approached the lighthouse, the first thing Aaryan noticed was the serenity of the place. It stood proudly against the open sea, with tall green mountains in the background, their peaks lightly kissed by passing clouds. The lighthouse itself was a simple but elegant structure—painted white with hints of rust from the years of standing against the ocean's relentless wind and salt.

They stepped out of the car, the gravel crunching softly beneath their shoes. The sky was a mix of grays and whites, a cloudy day typical of Langkawi's tropical climate, making the entire scene feel like a painting.

Aaryan took a deep breath. "This place feels untouched. Peaceful."

Maya nodded, gazing at the horizon where the ocean met the sky. "I love it when places aren't crowded. It's like the universe has reserved this moment just for us."

There were only two other people in sight—a man, possibly a local fisherman, standing by the rocky edge with a fishing rod, and another, sitting on one of the larger rocks, taking slow drags from a cigarette, lost in thought.

For an hour, Aaryan and Maya simply sat on the ground, their backs resting against a large rock, watching the waves roll in. They talked about life, their childhoods, and the places they had yet to see. It was one of those rare conversations where silence was as meaningful as the words spoken.

Leaving Perdana Quay Lighthouse behind, they continued their drive across the island. The roads in Langkawi were mesmerizingly flanked by rolling hills on one side and the endless ocean on the other.

"This doesn't feel real," Aaryan said, his eyes darting between the thick jungle-like greenery and the sparkling blue sea stretching far beyond. "It's like driving through a fantasy movie."

Maya smiled, rolling down her window. "Stick your hand out. Feel the wind."

Aaryan did as she said, stretching his arm out of the window. The cool breeze rushed past his skin, making him feel more alive than ever. Maya did the same, both of them letting the wind weave through their fingers as they sped down the winding roads of Langkawi. They stopped multiple times along the way, capturing photos of the scenic landscapes. Aaryan even made Maya pose in front of a row of coconut trees, teasing her about how her Instagram needed some "travel blogger" content.

Maya rolled her eyes. "I'd rather live the moment than post about it."

"Says the girl who takes fifty selfies before choosing one," Aaryan teased.

Maya punched his shoulder playfully, and they laughed, continuing their journey. Their next stop was an unassuming little restaurant—a humble, almost makeshift café nestled right on the beach. It had no extravagant signboard, no flashy decorations, just a few wooden tables and chairs placed directly on the sand, so close to the sea that waves occasionally lapped near their feet. They parked the car and walked down a short flight of stairs leading to the beach.

"Are you sure this place is open?" Aaryan asked, glancing around. There was only one staff member, an elderly man who looked like he had seen decades pass from this very spot.

Maya nodded. "It looks like self-service.

They ordered two shakes and sat down at a table closest to the water. Aaryan took his first sip, and his eyes widened in pure delight.

"This... this is hands down the best shake I've ever had."

Maya chuckled, a hint of triumph in her voice. "See? I knew you'd love it."

They sat there, sipping their shakes, their feet buried in the warm sand, watching the waves roll in and out like a gentle rhythm.

After finishing their drinks, they drove to Black Sand Beach, one of Langkawi's most fascinating natural wonders. As they stepped onto the shore, Aaryan was immediately captivated by the unusual dark texture of the sand. It wasn't pitch black but had deep charcoal streaks running through it, creating a mesmerizing pattern.

"Why is the sand black?" Aaryan asked.

Maya crossed her arms. "There's a legend behind it."

She paused for effect before continuing. "According to the myth, a battle took place between a Roman prince and a mermaid who lived in these waters. The mermaid was furious that humans had entered her territory, and in her anger, she cursed the beach, turning its sand black forever."

Aaryan chuckled. "That sounds like a fairy tale."

Maya shrugged. "Some say it's due to the high mineral content in the sand. But where's the fun in science?"

As much as he enjoyed the story, Aaryan was more interested in simply taking in the beauty of the place. The contrast between the black sand and the turquoise waters was something he had never seen before. Even Maya had never been to Langkawi, so she was equally surprised and in awe of its breathtaking scenery.

As evening approached, they made their way to the Kedawang Night Market in a small village. The market was alive with bright lights, sizzling sounds of food being cooked, and the chatter of locals and tourists alike. The aroma of grilled meats, fried snacks, and coconut rice filled the air. They sampled fried chicken and nasi lemak, a traditional Malaysian dish of fragrant rice cooked in coconut milk, served with sambal, anchovies, peanuts, and boiled eggs.

"This is heaven," Aaryan said, his mouth full.

Maya laughed and simply nodded, too busy enjoying her food to respond.

They ate their meals under the night sky, soaking in the vibrant yet relaxed energy of the market. By the time they returned to their resort, they were too full and too exhausted to do anything except crash on the beach. They borrowed beach towels from the staff, spread them on the sand, and lay side by side, gazing at the stars. The sky above was a vast ocean of twinkling lights, endless and mysterious. Maya slowly reached out and held Aaryan's hand.

"Thank you," she whispered.

Aaryan turned his head toward her. "For what?"

"For coming here. For making me forget."

Aaryan gently placed a finger on her lips. "Don't think about it. Just... be here. I'm with you."

Maya's gaze met Aaryan's, and in that silent exchange, they felt something deep and unspoken—an emotion beyond words, lingering somewhere between comfort and longing.

Was it love? Was it gratitude?

Could best friends be something more?

As those questions lingered in their minds, the waves continued their timeless dance against the shore, and the universe, as always, remained silent.

*****

The rising sun painted the ocean in shades of amber and gold, reflecting the rippling waves as they kissed the shoreline. The gentle rustling of palm trees and the distant chatter of birds formed the perfect melody to start another day in Langkawi. But for Maya and Aaryan, something had shifted between them. The unspoken emotions of the previous night still lingered in the air, weaving an invisible thread between them—something too fragile yet too powerful to ignore.

They met at the breakfast table, but unlike other mornings, their conversation was minimal. They weren't avoiding each other, but there was a newfound weight in the silence. Aaryan focused on the vast breakfast spread in front of him, stacking his plate with fresh tropical fruits, nasi lemak, and warm buttery croissants. Maya, on the other hand, stirred her coffee absentmindedly, her eyes occasionally drifting toward him.

Aaryan felt her gaze but chose not to look up. He had never felt this way before. Friendship had always been their foundation, but something deeper was creeping in, something neither of them could deny.

After a while, Maya finally spoke. "I think I won't be traveling too much today. Let's just spend some time in the resort, maybe read or do something alone."

Aaryan exhaled in relief. He had been thinking the same but didn't know how to bring it up. "Yeah, I think we need a break. It's been exhausting." He smiled briefly, still avoiding her eyes. "Let's just take it easy today."

Maya nodded, sipping her coffee. There was so much she wanted to say, but she didn't. Instead, she stood up and quietly walked away, heading toward her room.

That day, they spent their time apart, each lost in their own thoughts. They didn't do anything together—Aaryan went for a small walk around the resort, while Maya spent the day on the beach, letting the waves wash over her feet as she gazed at the horizon. It wasn't until evening that Aaryan returned to his room, feeling the weight of unspoken words between them.

Back in his room, Aaryan sat on the bed, staring at his phone. His parents had been calling him for two days, and he had been ignoring them, dreading the inevitable conversation. But today, he needed to talk. He needed clarity. Taking a deep breath, he dialed his mother's number. She picked up on the second ring.

"Aaryan! Where have you been? What are you up to?" His mother's voice was laced with worry and frustration.

"Ma... I need to tell you something." He hesitated for a second, then decided to just say it. "I think I'm in love with Maya. I want to marry her."

There was complete silence on the other end. Then, he heard muffled voices—his mother calling his father. Within seconds, his father was on the call.

"Aaryan, have you lost your mind?" His father's voice was stern. "Do you even understand what you are saying? She's dying, son! She won't be there for long. What will you do then?"

Aaryan clenched his fist. "I know, Papa. But that doesn't change how I feel about her. I love her. I want to be with her, no matter how long she has left."

His mother's voice was filled with desperation. "Beta, think about your future! You have your whole life ahead. What if you catch a disease from her? What about after she's gone? What will happen to you?"

"Ma!" Aaryan snapped, his voice shaking with emotion. "This is not about me. It's about her. I want to give her the happiest days of her life. If she only has months left, I want those months to be filled with love. With me."

"Aaryan, we won't allow this." His father's voice was firm.

"I wasn't asking for permission," Aaryan said, his voice steady. "I was looking for your blessings. But if I can't have them, I will do this on my own."

After a moment of silence, his mother's broken voice. "Beta... please, think once more."

"I already have, Ma." And with that, he ended the call.

Aaryan sat on the edge of his bed, his heart pounding. He had just made the biggest decision of his life—he loved Maya and wanted to marry her. Without wasting another second, he grabbed his phone and dialed her number. No answer. He called again. Still nothing. Panic surged through him. Jumping to his feet, he rushed out of his room and began searching the resort, his eyes scanning every corner. First, he ran toward her room, but she wasn't there. He ran past the pool, through the garden, and along the beachside restaurants—but she was nowhere to be seen. Then, he spotted something—a familiar figure near the beach shack, sitting alone in the sand, writing something with a wooden stick.

"Maya!" he shouted. "Maya!"

Maya flinched at the sound of his voice and quickly erased what she had written before turning around. She smiled nervously as Aaryan ran toward her, breathless.

She had been writing three words. *I love you, Aaryan.* But she wasn't ready to let him see it.

Aaryan dropped to his knees in front of her, taking her hands in his. His voice was trembling, but his eyes burned with intensity.

"Maya, you are my best friend. But it's more than that. I don't know why, but I want to marry you. I want to spend every single moment with you. I want to be the one you wake up to and the one you fall asleep beside. I love you, Maya."

Tears streamed down Maya's cheeks as she shook her head. "Aaryan... I love you too. More than anyone in this universe. But I won't marry you."

Aaryan's face fell. "Why not?"

"You have your whole life ahead, Aaryan," she whispered. "I don't want you to be left alone. I don't want you to suffer."

Aaryan cupped her face, his thumb wiping away her tears. "There is no point in a long life if I can't spend it with you. Even if it's just five months, I will live my entire life in those months. I only and only want to marry you, Maya."

Maya let out a shaky breath, her body trembling as she nodded. "Aaryan..."

"Say yes," Aaryan whispered.

She closed her eyes for a moment, then looked at him with a tearful smile. "Yes."

Aaryan didn't waste a second. He leaned in and pressed his lips to hers, softly at first, then deeper. Maya melted into him, letting go of all her fears.

That night, as the moon bathed Langkawi in its silver glow, Aaryan and Maya surrendered to the moment, letting the world outside fade into oblivion. The rhythmic crash of the waves against the shore became a melody, a silent witness to the love unfolding between them.

Back in their room, there was no need for words—silence carried more meaning than anything they could say. Aaryan's fingers traced the delicate curves of Maya's body with a tenderness that made her shiver. He wasn't just touching her; he was memorizing her, as if committing every inch of her to his soul. And for the first time in a long time, Maya felt truly alive. There was no pain, no sickness—only love.

They held each other close, their bodies entwined, their breaths merging as one. Aaryan kissed her deeply, his lips lingering, savoring the taste of her. His hands caressed her softly, moving with a reverence that spoke of love, not just passion. Maya, overwhelmed by the intensity of the moment, ran her fingers through his hair, whispering his name like a sacred prayer.

Hours passed, but time held no meaning. Wrapped in each other's warmth, neither of them wanted to let go.

Even when exhaustion finally claimed them, they remained connected, their hearts beating in perfect harmony.

Maya rested her head on Aaryan's chest, listening to the steady rhythm of his heartbeat—a comforting lullaby in the quiet night.

"Aaryan?" she whispered.

"Hmm?" His voice was drowsy yet tender.

"Thank you for loving me."

Aaryan pressed a gentle kiss on her forehead. "I always will."

As she drifted off to sleep in his arms, a profound sense of peace enveloped her. In that moment, she knew—this was the happiest night of her life.

*****

The golden rays of the morning sun filtered through the sheer white curtains of their resort room in Langkawi. The scent of ocean breeze lingered in the air. Maya stirred slightly, trying to move, but Aaryan's arm was wrapped tightly around her waist, his grip possessive, his body still warm against hers.

She giggled softly and whispered, "Aaryan, are you planning to strangle me in your sleep?"

He tightened his hold and nuzzled against her shoulder, murmuring, "I'm never letting you go."

Maya turned to face him, her fingers brushing against his stubble. "And what are your intentions now, mister?"

Aaryan's eyes opened slightly, a mischievous glint in them. He leaned in and captured her lips in a slow, lingering kiss, deepening it as his hands moved along her back. "This," he whispered against her lips.

Maya gasped as he rolled her onto her back, his lips trailing down her neck. The morning light bathed their skin in a warm glow as they made love once more, their movements unhurried, savoring each touch, each whisper, each kiss.

Afterward, they lay in each other's arms, breathing in sync. Maya traced circles on Aaryan's chest and said, "We need to get up, or we'll miss breakfast."

Aaryan groaned, pulling her back into his arms. "Five more minutes."

But Maya was already out of bed, playfully throwing a pillow at him. "Come on, lazy! We have a journey ahead."

They showered together, laughter and playful kisses filling the steamy bathroom before they quickly got dressed and headed to the resort restaurant for breakfast. After breakfast, they packed their bags and drove toward the ferry terminal. The journey back to Kuala Kedah was familiar, the wind whipping through their hair as they reminisced about their time in Langkawi.

As soon as they reached Kuala Kedah, they set off on a drive toward George Town, Penang, a mere 90-minute voyage. Aaryan, sitting in the passenger seat, held Maya's hand, occasionally lifting it to press soft kisses against her knuckles.

"So, tell me about Penang," Aaryan asked, tracing small circles on her palm.

Maya smiled. "It's completely different from Langkawi. You'll feel like you've stepped into another world. Penang is known for its colonial architecture, street art, and, of course, its legendary food. People from Singapore and Thailand even fly here just for the food."

Aaryan raised an eyebrow. "It must be something special, then."

"You'll see," Maya said with a playful smirk.

Soon, the roads led them into the heart of George Town. Aaryan's eyes widened in amazement as he took in the surroundings—majestic colonial-era buildings, vibrant murals covering old shophouses, and a blend of Chinese temples, mosques, and churches, all standing in harmony.

"Wow," he whispered, stepping out of the car. "It feels like I just traveled back in time. This place is mesmerizing."

Maya chuckled. "I knew you'd love it."

They checked into a heritage hotel, an old, restored mansion with wooden beams and intricate Peranakan-style tiles. As they stood at the reception, Maya turned to the staff and confidently said, "One room."

Aaryan blushed, looking away, but Maya caught his reaction and winked at him.

As soon as they entered the room, Maya tossed her bag on the bed and grabbed a small pouch. She took out a handful of pills and swallowed them with water.

Aaryan frowned. "This many medicines?"

Maya met his gaze. "These keep me alive. If I don't take them, I won't be able to move or feel fresh. They help me keep up with all this exertion."

Aaryan hesitated before asking, "Will they not... cure your disease?"

Maya's smile faltered. "No cure. These are just for a painless death."

Aaryan's heart clenched. He immediately pulled her into his arms. "You are not dying, Maya. You will live. You will live."

She closed her eyes, breathing in his warmth, his determination. She wished he was right.

Determined not to let the moment become heavy, Maya grabbed Aaryan's hand and led him out of their hotel room. The warm air greeted them as they stepped onto the bustling streets of George Town.

"We're starting with Penang's best dishes," she announced.

They stopped at a small hawker stall tucked away on a bustling street corner. The place had a rustic charm, with wooden tables, colorful plastic chairs, and the hum of conversation filling the air. The scent of sizzling woks and fragrant spices drifted from the open-air cooking station, where an elderly vendor moved with practiced ease, ladling steaming broth into bowls.

They ordered Hokkien Mee, a fragrant prawn noodle soup served piping hot in deep bowls. The rich, orange-hued broth shimmered under the midday sun, its aroma thick with the scent of slow-cooked prawns and spices. Maya requested yellow noodles with extra prawns, and as they took their seats at a shaded table, the heat of the dish mixed with the warmth of the afternoon air.

Aaryan took his first sip of the broth, letting the deep, umami-rich flavor settle on his tongue. He exhaled in appreciation. "This is incredible—spicy, flavorful, just the right kick." He eagerly picked up the noodles, slurping them up with a satisfied sigh.

Maya grinned. "Told you it's a must-try."

Next came Char Kway Teow—stir-fried flat rice noodles, glistening with oil and tossed with prawns, Chinese sausages, and cockles. The hawker expertly flipped the noodles in a scorching hot wok, filling the air with an irresistible smoky aroma. Aaryan grabbed his chopsticks and took a bite. The combination of silky noodles, crunchy bean sprouts, and juicy prawns made him pause, savoring the layers of flavor.

"This... this is unreal," he said, shaking his head in amazement. "The smokiness, the textures—this might be my new favorite dish."

Maya laughed, enjoying his enthusiasm. "You always say that after every meal here."

From an adjoining stall, Maya ordered Chendol, a cooling bowl of shaved ice topped with green rice flour jelly, red beans, and thick palm sugar syrup. The icy sweetness was perfect for the humid afternoon. Aaryan took a spoonful, letting the syrup coat his tongue before making a face.

Maya smirked. "Too sweet?"

He nodded, pushing the bowl toward her. "I think I'll leave dessert to you."

She laughed, happily finishing his portion while Aaryan leaned back in his chair, satisfied and already looking forward to their next food adventure.

"Where does all this food go?" Aaryan teased.

Maya patted her stomach playfully. "Straight to my happiness."

After indulging in a delicious meal, they made their way to one of Penang's most iconic attractions, Penang Hill. In the late afternoon, they boarded a tram that slowly ascended the steep hillside, revealing a breathtaking panorama of the city below. As they climbed higher, the air turned cooler, offering a refreshing contrast to the humid afternoon heat.

Dense rainforest enveloped them, the towering trees forming a lush green canopy that occasionally parted to reveal glimpses of the shimmering coastline in the distance. Birds chirped in the foliage, their calls blending with the steady rumble of the tram, adding to the peaceful atmosphere.

When they finally reached the top, the view was nothing short of spectacular. The entire island stretched out before them, bathed in golden sunlight as the afternoon began to wane. The skyscrapers of George Town stood proudly in the distance, their glass facades glinting under the sun, while the coastline curved elegantly along the horizon. Wisps of clouds hovered over the distant hills, adding to the dreamlike beauty of the scene.

“Look at this view,” Aaryan whispered, awestruck. “It’s marvelous.”

Maya leaned against the railing, inhaling deeply, savoring the crisp mountain air. “Sometimes, it’s not the place. It’s the person you see it with.”

Aaryan turned to her, warmth spreading through his chest. He reached for her hand, giving it a gentle squeeze. “I couldn’t agree more.”

They wandered along the pathways, taking their time to explore the hill’s many charms. The colonial-era building, remnant of British rule, stood gracefully among the trees, it’s white walls and red-tiled roofs adding to the hill’s old-world charm. They stopped at the viewing deck, where a telescope allowed them to zoom in on the city below. Aaryan playfully pointed it toward random spots, pretending to search for hidden treasures, making Maya laugh.

As the afternoon drifted toward evening, they made their way to Kek Lok Si Temple, one of the largest and most magnificent Buddhist temples in Southeast Asia. From afar, the temple complex was a mesmerizing sight, its multi-tiered pagodas rising against the sky. As they approached, the grandeur of the temple became even more evident—the intricate carvings, the vibrant murals, and the sheer size of the complex left them in awe.

The first thing that caught Aaryan's attention was the towering statue of the Goddess of Mercy, Kuan Yin, standing gracefully atop the hill. The bronze figure, nearly 100 feet tall, radiated a sense of serenity and wisdom, her calm gaze seeming to watch over the island. Around the base of the statue, golden prayer wheels spun gently in the breeze, each inscribed with sacred mantras.

They wandered through the temple's many halls, admiring the elaborate altars adorned with golden Buddha statues. Monks in saffron robes moved quietly, some in prayer, others tending to offerings of fresh flowers and incense. Maya led Aaryan to the famous Pagoda of Ten Thousand Buddhas, an architectural marvel blending Chinese, Thai, and Burmese styles. The walls were lined with countless small Buddha figurines, each intricately detailed.

The scent of burning incense filled the air as they paused at a prayer pavilion. Maya lit a stick of incense, clasping her hands together in silent reverence. Aaryan watched her for a moment before doing the same, allowing the serene atmosphere to wash over him.

As the sun dipped below the horizon, the temple transformed. Rows of red and gold lanterns flickered to life, casting a warm, ethereal glow over the sacred grounds. The entire complex seemed to shimmer under the soft lights, creating a scene straight out of a dream.

Maya sighed, taking it all in. “This is one of my favorite places.”

Aaryan looked at her, the temple’s golden glow reflecting in her eyes. He reached for her hand, intertwining his fingers with hers. “Mine too, now.”

They stood there for a while, savoring the moment—the stillness, the beauty, and the quiet understanding that this day, this experience, would stay with them forever.

On their way back to the hotel, they strolled through the lively streets, the night air carrying the scent of sizzling food and spices. Aaryan suddenly tugged Maya’s hand, his eyes lighting up as he spotted a street cart selling Char Kway Teow.

“We have to stop,” he insisted. “I can’t leave Penang without having it again.”

Maya laughed but happily agreed. They ordered a plate, watching as the vendor expertly tossed the flat rice noodles in the sizzling wok, adding prawns, Chinese sausages, and crunchy bean sprouts. The smoky aroma was irresistible.

Aaryan took his first bite and sighed in satisfaction. “Still the best thing I’ve ever eaten.”

Maya shook her head, amused. "You're officially addicted."

As they shared the plate under the glow of streetlights, surrounded by the pulse of the city, the day felt complete—full of adventure, laughter, and flavors they would never forget.

Back at the hotel, exhaustion weighed on them, but the moment they stepped into their room, an irresistible spark ignited between them.

Maya stood near the window, gazing at the twinkling city lights. Aaryan walked up behind her, wrapping his arms around her waist. "Tired?" he murmured against her neck.

She turned in his embrace, looking into his eyes. "Not too tired."

Aaryan's lips met hers, slow and deep, igniting a fire between them. He lifted her effortlessly, carrying her to bed, their bodies molding together like two halves of a whole. They undressed each other with unhurried tenderness, as if savoring every inch of skin revealed. Aaryan traced soft kisses along Maya's collarbone, down to her stomach, whispering how beautiful she was. Maya pulled him closer, their bodies moving in perfect harmony, lost in the rhythm of love. It wasn't just physical, it was an unspoken promise, a desperate need to hold onto the moment, to cherish every second.

Later, as they lay tangled in each other's arms, their breathing slowing, Aaryan kissed Maya's forehead.

"I love you," he whispered.

Maya pressed her face into his chest. "I love you too."

As sleep claimed them, wrapped in warmth and love, neither wanted the night to end.

*****

The next morning was bright, and the scent of freshly brewed coffee and baked pastries filled the air in the hotel's breakfast area. Maya and Aaryan sat across from each other, their fingers occasionally brushing as they reached for the same dish. It was a quiet, slow morning—just how they had decided to keep it.

Maya smiled at Aaryan as she lifted her cup of tea. "This might be the first time we're having breakfast without rushing somewhere right after."

Aaryan chuckled, spreading butter on his toast. "Well, you deserve a slow day. No running around, no long drives. Just peace."

Just as he finished speaking, he noticed Maya's expression change. Her smile faded, her eyes fluttered, and before he could react, her body swayed and collapsed onto the floor.

"Maya!" Aaryan shouted, his chair screeching as he pushed it back and ran to her. He held her head in his lap, his hands trembling as he lightly tapped her cheek. "Maya, wake up. Maya!"

Panic gripped his heart as the restaurant staff gathered around them. He looked up, his voice urgent. "Call an ambulance! Now!"

One of the staff members rushed toward the reception, and within minutes, the sound of sirens echoed through the air. The paramedics arrived swiftly, carefully placing Maya on a stretcher and carrying her into the ambulance. Aaryan sat beside her, holding her cold hand as they sped through the streets of George Town toward

Penang General Hospital. The moment they arrived, Maya was rushed into the emergency room, disappearing behind swinging double doors. The waiting room felt suffocating. Aaryan paced back and forth, his fingers tangled in his hair, his mind racing. He had never felt this helplessness before.

Minutes felt like hours until finally, a nurse approached him. "Are you with Miss Maya?"

"Yes," he answered instantly.

"Please come in."

He rushed inside and found Maya lying on a hospital bed, looking pale but awake. Relief washed over him, but his heart still ached seeing her like this.

A doctor stood beside her, flipping through her medical records. "Mr. Aaryan, she collapsed due to excessive exertion. She needs to rest!"

Maya, her voice soft but steady, said, "I'm fine, Aaryan. It's just my body reminding me that it's running out of time."

Aaryan clenched his jaw, shaking his head. "Don't say that. You're not running out of time. You're just tired, that's all."

The doctor advised rest and discharged Maya by evening. Aaryan helped her into a taxi and brought her back to the hotel. As soon as they entered the room, Aaryan guided Maya to the bed and helped her sit. He knelt in front of her, taking her hand and placing a gentle kiss on her palm.

"You scared me today, Maya." His voice was barely above a whisper.

Maya managed a weak smile. "I didn't mean to."

Aaryan cupped her face. "I don't want to risk losing you. Enough of the travel. We should just stay in Kuala Lumpur for the rest of the days."

Maya's expression shifted. She pulled her hands away and looked down, her eyes glistening. "Wouldn't you let me live my dream, Aaryan? Would you want me to die without realizing it?" Her voice broke, and tears spilled onto her cheeks.

Aaryan's heart ached seeing her in pain. He moved closer, holding her trembling hands. "I came all the way here, leaving everything behind, just to see my best friend's dream come true. We'll do everything you wish, but we'll have to slow down. No more exhausting journeys. Just gentle, peaceful trips. Okay?"

Maya wiped her tears and nodded. She leaned against Aaryan's chest, feeling the steady beat of his heart. "Sleep beside me," she murmured.

Aaryan climbed onto the bed, letting her rest her head on his chest. He stroked her hair until her breathing steadied, her body relaxing in his arms.

The next morning, Maya woke up feeling stronger, while Aaryan felt more hopeful. They didn't rush to get ready. Instead, they took their time, heading to the breakfast area at a leisurely pace. They talked over coffee, reminiscing about their journey so far.

"I'm so grateful that you came for me, Aaryan," Maya said, looking into his eyes.

Aaryan smiled, shaking his head. "I should be the one thanking you. You came into my life first as my best friend, and now, you're my everything."

As they continued eating, Aaryan suddenly brought up the topic of marriage. "Maya, we should start planning our wedding now."

Maya's eyes sparkled with excitement. "Really?" she said, her voice filled with joy. "That's wonderful, Aaryan! We should start planning everything right away! I'm already imagining myself looking like a princess in my wedding gown. You know, Aaryan, when I was a kid, I would always dream of wearing that gown one day whenever I was at someone's wedding."

Aaryan laughed. "And I suppose that makes me your prince?"

She nodded eagerly. "Of course! You'd look dashing in a suit."

"Where should we do it?" Aaryan asked.

Maya smiled softly; her eyes filled with longing. "I've always wanted to get married in Malacca."

Aaryan nodded, a warm smile spreading across his face. "Sounds perfect."

Maya then hesitated. "But... who would come? I might have three or four friends... maybe no one."

Aaryan admitted sadly, "My parents won't come. So, from my side, no one either."

Maya squeezed his hand. "We don't need anyone. We have each other."

Aaryan smiled. "That's enough for me."

After the previous day's incident, Maya was supposed to rest, but she had one great desire—to visit Batu Ferringhi, a peaceful beach she had dreamed of since childhood. They reached there in about 40 minutes, stopping by a small food stall to grab burgers before heading toward a wooden bench near the shore, away from the bright sun and crashing waves.

Aaryan looked around in awe. "This is one of the most beautiful places I've ever seen."

Maya smiled. "I've wanted to come here since I was a little girl. I used to see pictures of this place and imagine myself sitting here, watching the waves."

Aaryan took a deep breath, feeling the ocean breeze. "Tell me about your childhood."

Maya leaned back against the bench. "I was always a dreamer. I wanted to travel, to explore. "My parents were strict, wanting me to succeed in life, and we didn't have much money. So, I wasn't allowed much freedom. But I would read books and imagine myself in different places."

Aaryan chuckled. "I can picture you as a little girl, stubborn and full of dreams."

She grinned. "Oh, I was stubborn, alright. What about you?"

Aaryan confessed, looking at the waves. "My parents never forced me to do much, but they were strict about certain things they wouldn't compromise on. We were a middle-class family—didn't have many luxuries, but we lived decently. I never dreamt too much."

Maya reached for his hand. "But you're here now. And you're making my dream come true."

Aaryan clutched her hand. "And you made me realize that I can dream too."

They sat there for hours, talking, laughing, and watching the sun dip below the horizon.

"As the sky turned shades of orange and pink, Maya rested her head on Aaryan's shoulder and whispered, 'Let's go back.'"

Aaryan nodded. "Let's go."

Hand in hand, they walked back, carrying with them memories, promises, and a love that would defy time itself.

*****

The journey from Penang to Cameron Highlands began early in the morning on the next day. Maya was brimming with excitement, her eyes twinkling with the same joy as a child on their first trip to an amusement park. For years, she had dreamt of visiting this place.

She leaned her head against the car seat, watching the scenery shift outside the window. "Do you know, Aaryan?" she said, her voice filled with nostalgia. "I've been drinking Cameron Highlands tea since I was a little girl. My family would always buy tea grown in the Cameron Highlands. I grew up imagining what this place would look like. And today... we're actually going there."

Aaryan, his hand on the steering wheel, glanced at her and smiled. "Then I guess today is another dream coming true for you, Maya."

She nodded, her fingers tracing the car window as the landscapes changed.

The drive was long—about four hours—but breathtaking. As they ascended higher into the mountains, the air grew cooler. The roads had sharp bends, but the beauty surrounding them made every turn worth it. The greenery stretched endlessly, clouds gently kissing the mountain peaks. A cool breeze filtered through the car windows, carrying the fresh scent of wet earth and tea plantations. They stopped multiple times along the way—sometimes to take pictures, sometimes just to breathe in the crisp mountain air. One of their stops was at a tea estate that stretched as far as the eye could see.

Maya stepped out of the car, closing her eyes and inhaling deeply. "This... this is what I always imagined," she whispered.

Aaryan stood beside her, watching her soak in the moment. "You always dreamed of coming here. And now, you finally have."

She turned to him and held his hand. "And it's even better because you're here with me."

They continued their journey, reaching Brinchang by afternoon. The small town had a charm of its own—mist-covered roads, wooden houses, and a local market bustling with vendors selling warm street food and handmade crafts. Upon arrival, they checked into their hotel, a cozy lodge nestled against the hillside. The wooden interiors and large windows overlooking the tea plantations gave the place a rustic charm. After a brief rest, they freshened up and set out to explore the town, eager to take in the cool mountain air and lively atmosphere.

The moment they stepped into the local market, Maya shivered. She wasn't wearing warm clothes, and the cool highland breeze nipped at her skin. Without hesitation, she hugged Aaryan tightly as they wandered through the marketplace.

Aaryan chuckled, rubbing her arms to warm her up. "You should have brought something warm, stubborn woman."

Maya looked up at him with an innocent pout. "I didn't know it would be this cold!"

Shaking his head, Aaryan pulled her towards a small shop selling woolen clothes. He picked a pullover and slipped it over her head. "There, now you're warm."

Maya grinned. "And you?"

"I'll get one too," he said, picking another pullover for himself.

They spent a little more time exploring the market before heading to a small street stall for a meal. The steam from a bowl of laksa curled into the air, its rich aroma filling their nostrils.

Maya took a spoonful of the hot broth and sighed happily. "This is perfect for a chilly evening."

Aaryan took a bite of the noodles, nodding in agreement. "Definitely. Spicy, warm, and comforting."

After dinner, they retired early to their hotel cozy mansion perched on the hilltop. The room had an old-world charm with wooden flooring, a fireplace, and large windows that overlooked the valley below. Aaryan helped Maya onto the bed, her exhaustion evident. Without a word, he sat behind her and began massaging her shoulders, his fingers kneading her tense muscles.

She let out a small sigh of relief. "That feels so good, Aaryan."

"You need it," he murmured, continuing his gentle movements.

For an hour, he massaged her back, shoulders, and arms until she felt relaxed. Maya, feeling the warmth of his touch, slowly drifted into sleep, resting her head on his lap. Aaryan leaned back, his fingers still tangled in her hair, and soon, he dozed off as well.

The next morning, they woke up early, filled with excitement. Today was the day Maya had waited all her life—the day she would visit the Boh Tea Plantation. The drive to the tea estate was breathtaking. Rolling green hills stretched endlessly, covered in meticulously planted tea bushes that created a beautiful, rhythmic pattern. As they approached, the crisp mountain air carried the scent of fresh tea leaves.

Maya's eyes sparkled as she stepped out of the car. "This... this is my heaven, Aaryan."

They walked through the plantation, watching workers skillfully pluck tea leaves. Aaryan listened intently as Maya explained the process of tea production, her voice animated with passion.

"Did you know," she said, pointing to a section of the plantation, "the tea bushes here are pruned regularly to maintain their size? It makes harvesting easier."

Aaryan smiled, amused by how much she knew. "I swear, you sound like a tour guide."

She laughed. "I've read about this place all my life. I know almost everything!"

Excited to explore, they visited the tea factory, where they observed how the leaves were processed, dried, and packaged. The aroma inside was intoxicating. After the tour, they headed to the Boh Tea Centre, a modern café overlooking the lush valley. They ordered a selection of teas and pastries.

Maya took a sip of her tea, closing her eyes. "This is the best tea I've ever had."

Aaryan leaned back, gazing at the stunning view. "I think this might be the best view of our trip so far."

They sat there quietly, occasionally whispering about the beauty of the place and the people around them. For Maya, it was a dream come true. And for Aaryan, it was a moment he would treasure forever. By early evening, they visited the strawberry farm. Rows upon rows of bright red strawberries stretched across the farm, their crisp fragrance drifting through the air.

Maya's excitement was contagious. "I've never been so close to nature, Aaryan. I grew up in a city, surrounded by concrete buildings. This... this is magical."

They were given small baskets and allowed to pluck their own strawberries.

Maya giggled as she carefully selected the ripest ones. "I feel like a farmer!"

Aaryan smirked. "You look like one too, crouching like that."

She stuck her tongue out at him and continued picking. Once their baskets were full, they bought a few strawberry-flavored treats before heading back to town. That night, they visited the Brinchang Night Market, a bustling hub of food stalls, bright lights, and the irresistible scent of sizzling street food. The air was thick with the smoky aroma of grilled meats and spices as vendors skillfully flipped skewers over open flames and tossed noodles in sizzling woks.

For their final meal of the day, they decided on chicken—succulent, marinated meat skewers grilled to perfection over a charcoal fire. Each skewer was coated in a rich, slightly charred peanut sauce, its nutty sweetness balanced by a hint of spice. Aaryan took a bite, savoring the tenderness of the meat and the burst of flavors.

"This is incredible," he murmured between bites. "Smoky, juicy, and that sauce—absolutely perfect."

Maya dipped her skewer into more sauce. “Told you, the satay here is on another level.”

They also ordered mee goreng ayam, a plate of stir-fried noodles tossed with tender chicken, crisp vegetables, and a spicy, savory sauce. The dish was topped with a fried egg, its golden yolk running over the steaming noodles as Maya mixed it in.

Aaryan took a mouthful, his eyes widening at the explosion of flavors. “This has the right amount of heat,” he said, enjoying the balance of spice and umami. “And the egg just makes it even better.”

Maya nodded, slurping up a noodle. “Nothing beats a good plate of mee goreng on a cool night.”

They ate slowly, savoring every bite, the lively market atmosphere adding to the experience. By the time they finished, they felt warm, full, and utterly satisfied, the perfect ending to a day filled with adventure and flavors they wouldn’t soon forget. Back in their room, Maya sat beside Aaryan, massaging his shoulders.

"You always take care of me," she whispered. "Tonight, let me take care of you."

Aaryan closed his eyes, enjoying her touch. But soon, her hands trailed down his arms, her lips pressing softly against his neck. The air between them changed slowly, intimately, filled with unspoken emotions.

Maya looked up at him, her eyes searching his. "Stay with me tonight—just hold me."

Aaryan gently cradled her face, pressing a deep, slow kiss to her lips. Their bodies moved closer, their heartbeats syncing. There was no urgency—just a slow, passionate exploration of love, warmth, and emotion. Wrapped in each other's embrace, they drifted into sleep, their bodies entwined, their hearts beating as one.

*****

Next day in the afternoon, they started their journey back to Kuala Lumpur. The drive from Cameron Highlands to Kuala Lumpur was slow and unhurried. Aaryan made sure of that. Maya was no longer the same girl who had started this journey with him. She had lost three kilos, maybe more. Her face, once glowing with life, had grown paler. Her hands, once warm and full of energy, felt frail in his. But if there was one thing that remained unchanged, it was her spirit.

Aaryan had noticed every little change in her, but he never let her see his concern. Instead, he always told her how beautiful she looked. Not because he wanted to give her false hope, but because he truly believed it. He loved her with all his heart and in these last days, that love had only deepened. She dozed off halfway through the journey, her head resting against the window. Aaryan glanced at her from time to time, his heart aching yet swelling with love. He had given up everything to be by her side. He had no expectations, no selfish desires, just a wish to see her happy, to make her every moment worthwhile. They made a brief stop at a small roadside café. The place was quiet, nestled amidst lush greenery, with wooden tables and chairs scattered outside.

Maya stirred awake as the car came to a halt. "Where are we?" she asked, rubbing her eyes.

"Just a small café by the road," Aaryan said. "Thought we could use a break—and some coffee."

Maya smiled. "You know me too well."

They sat across from each other, savoring their steaming coffee. Its rich aroma drifted through the air, blending with the crisp, earthy scent left behind by the night's rain.

Maya wrapped her fingers around the warm cup. "Aaryan..." she began softly.

"Hmm?"

"You're happy with me, right?"

He looked at her, his eyes filled with nothing but love. "What kind of question is that?" He reached out and took her hand in his. "I have never been happier in my life, Maya."

She gave a small, contented smile. "Good. Because I want you to remember this forever."

Aaryan didn't respond immediately; he just held her hand a little tighter. They finished their coffee in comfortable silence before continuing their drive. By the time they reached Kuala Lumpur, the sun was beginning to set, casting a warm glow over the city skyline.

Over the next four days, they took things slowly, savoring their time together. On the first day, Aaryan had a special idea in mind.

"Maya," he said as they sat in her apartment, "let's go to the top of the Petronas Towers."

Maya's breath hitched in surprise. "Really?"

"Yes," Aaryan nodded. "I've never been to such a tall building before."

She nodded, a soft look in her eyes. "Even I could never afford it before. Coming from a poor background, going to a place like that felt like a dream too far away. And when I had money, I didn't have time."

Aaryan stood up, held out his hand, and said, "Then let's make that dream come true today."

She took his hand, and together, they made their way to the iconic towers. As Aaryan approached the Petronas Towers, a wave of disbelief washed over him. They were breathtaking, almost surreal—as if they belonged to another world. The moment they stepped into the elevator, Maya's excitement was almost childlike. As they ascended to the top, she held onto Aaryan's arm tightly.

When they finally reached the Skybridge, she let out a gasp. "Aaryan... this is... breathtaking."

They stood at the glass windows, looking at the vast city below. Skyscrapers stretched far and wide, cars moved like tiny ants, and the evening lights of Kuala Lumpur flickered like stars.

Maya turned to Aaryan. "Thank you."

"For what?"

"For making every little dream of mine come true."

Aaryan gently brushed a strand of hair from her face. "You deserve this and more, Maya."

They took pictures together, capturing the moment forever. Then, hand in hand, they descended and headed for lunch. For lunch, they stopped at a traditional Nasi Kandar restaurant. The aroma of rich curries and fragrant rice filled the air.

Aaryan looked at the menu, slightly confused. "What exactly is Nasi Kandar?"

Maya chuckled. "It's a Malaysian dish with Indian roots. The name comes from the old days when Indian-

Muslim vendors carried rice and curry in baskets balanced on a pole over their shoulders— 'nasi' means rice, and 'kandar' means shoulder."

"So, what should I try?" Aaryan asked.

Maya pointed at her plate. "This. Steamed rice with a mix of different curries—fish, chicken, and beef. You pour them all together. It's a flavor explosion!"

Aaryan did as she said, mixing the curries, letting the rich aroma of spices rise to him. As he took the first bite, a shock flashed across his face—his taste buds instantly awakened by the bold, complex flavors. The blend of savory, spicy, and slightly tangy gravies coated the rice perfectly, each bite bursting with depth.

"Wow. This is incredible!" he exclaimed, savoring the mix of fragrant rice and aromatic curries.

"Told you!" she said with a victorious grin, watching his expression of pure satisfaction.

They spent the rest of the meal talking about the cultural blend of Malaysia, how food told stories, and how even the simplest dishes carried history within them. That evening, they wandered through Bukit Bintang, the heartbeat of Kuala Lumpur's nightlife. Street musicians played rock music at the corners. Groups of young dancers entertained the crowd with their moves. The streets were alive with tourists, food stalls, and neon lights flashing in every direction.

Maya held Aaryan's hand. "It feels good to be back in the city for a while, doesn't it?"

"Yeah," he agreed, looking around. "We've been surrounded by nature for so long, I almost forgot what a big city felt like."

They roamed for hours, absorbing the energy of the place. The noise, the lights, the people, it was a stark contrast to the quiet beaches and mountains they had been exploring. But tonight, it felt perfect. By the time they returned to Maya's apartment, exhaustion had settled in.

As they lay in bed, Aaryan whispered, "Maya, about our wedding"

But before he could finish, she had already drifted into sleep in his arms.

He smiled, kissed her forehead, and whispered, "We'll talk tomorrow, my love." With that, the night embraced them in its quiet serenity.

The next morning, Maya woke up feeling better than she had in days. She stretched, made a cup of coffee, and handed one to Aaryan, who was still in bed.

"Wake up, sleepyhead," she said playfully. She sat beside him on the couch, sipping her own.

He smiled. "You know, we didn't finish our discussion last night."

Maya's eyes twinkled. "Yes, we didn't." She placed her coffee on the table, took Aaryan's hands in hers, and said, "Aaryan, let's get married next week."

Aaryan's heart swelled with emotion. "Are you sure?"

She nodded. "I don't want to wait anymore. I don't care if it's grand or simple. I just want to be yours."

Aaryan gently held her face, his eyes searching hers. "You already are mine, Maya. You always have been."

She leaned in, resting her forehead against his. "Then let's do it. Let's get married in Melaka."

Aaryan kissed her softly. "Okay. Let's do it."

And in that moment, a promise was made—not just of marriage, but of love, devotion, and a lifetime of memories, no matter how long or short that life would be.

*****

The apartment in Kuala Lumpur had become their little sanctuary. Aaryan and Maya spent most of their time inside, either curled up on the couch talking about the future or simply enjoying the comfort of each other's presence. They ordered food from nearby vendors, sometimes trying something new, sometimes sticking to their favorites. The days were slow, but they cherished them.

One afternoon, as they sat on the balcony sipping coffee, Aaryan leaned back in his chair, gazing at the city skyline. "You know, I've decided something."

Maya looked at him, amused. "What is it?"

"From now on, I'll be eating Malaysian food in India too."

Maya chuckled. "That's great! But where will you get it from? It's not like Malaysian food is available everywhere in India."

Aaryan sighed dramatically. "Exactly my problem! Who will cook it for me?"

Maya smirked. "Oh baby, I'll teach you. Don't worry."

Aaryan smiled, then reached out for her hand. "Okay, at least one dish you teach me so that I can eat it every day and remember you."

The moment he said that his voice faltered, and his eyes filled with tears. He hadn't meant to say it like that, but the reality hit him—he was preparing for a life where Maya wouldn't be by his side.

Maya, instead of breaking down, simply smiled and jumped onto his lap, wrapping her arms around his neck.

"No tears," she whispered, pressing a soft kiss against his lips. "I don't want you to cry for me. Not now, not ever."

Aaryan held her tightly. "I just wish... I wish I could keep you forever."

Maya pulled back slightly, cupping his face. "Aaryan, I have already accepted my fate. And I don't want to spend these days thinking about what I can't change. I only have two dreams left—our wedding and Melaka. Nothing more, nothing less."

Aaryan nodded, swallowing his emotions. "Then we'll make them both perfect."

Maya grinned. "Yes, we will."

That evening, as they lay on the couch, Aaryan pulled out his phone and began searching for Melaka. He had read about it before, but now he wanted to know everything.

Maya raised an eyebrow. "What are you up to?"

Aaryan smirked. "I'm just curious about Melaka. It seems like my kind of place—creative, laid-back, filled with history."

She chuckled. "That's why I wanted to take you there."

That night, they lay in bed, discussing every little detail of their wedding.

"The dress?" Maya asked.

Aaryan thought for a moment. "Something elegant but simple. Maybe white or silver?"

Maya nodded. "I like silver. With some shine on it."

"And for me?" Aaryan asked playfully.

"A light grey three-piece suit," Maya said without hesitation. "It'll suit you."

Aaryan smiled. "Done."

They planned everything—the venue, the vows, the little things that would make their wedding uniquely theirs. And for the first time in days, there was no sadness, no fear. Only excitement for what was to come.

The next morning, they woke up with one mission—to get everything they needed for their wedding. Their first stop was Suria KLCC Mall, one of the most luxurious malls in Kuala Lumpur. Aaryan had insisted on taking Maya to the best place possible. As they entered the bridal boutique, Maya's eyes sparkled.

"Oh my God, Aaryan, look at this place!" she whispered excitedly.

Rows of exquisite wedding gowns filled the store, each one more beautiful than the last.

Aaryan smiled. "Go on, try whatever you like."

Maya took her time, looking through the collection. Finally, her eyes landed on a silver gown adorned with delicate shiny stones.

"This one," she whispered, touching the fabric.

Aaryan took one look at it and nodded. "It's perfect."

Maya tried it on, and when she stepped out of the fitting room, Aaryan's breath caught in his throat.

"You look... stunning," he said, completely mesmerized.

Maya twirled. "You think so?"

Aaryan walked up to her and gently held her waist. "I know so."

They bought the gown, and next, it was Aaryan's turn. Maya found him a light grey three-piece traditional suit.

When he tried it on, Maya beamed. "Now you look like my groom."

He smirked. "Always have been."

After purchasing their outfits, they moved to the jewelry store to buy their wedding rings.

Aaryan held up a simple yet elegant silver band. "This one?"

Maya nodded. "Yes. It's beautiful."

They purchased the rings, along with a pair of formal shoes for Aaryan and high heels for Maya. Despite Maya's protest, Aaryan insisted on paying.

Aaryan shook his head. "Nope. This is my treat. Our wedding, my responsibility."

Maya smiled and rolled her eyes. "You and your old-school ways."

By the time they returned to the apartment, they were fatigued but filled with excitement. That evening, they sat in the living room, holding hands.

"Let's practice our vows," Maya suggested.

Aaryan chuckled. "You're really taking this seriously."

"Of course!" Maya said. "We need to do this right."

Aaryan took her hand formally. "Maya, from the moment I met you, my life changed in ways I never imagined. You are my love, my strength, and my forever.

Today, I promise to stand by you, to love you endlessly, and to cherish every moment with you."

Maya's eyes softened. "That was perfect."

"Your turn," Aaryan said.

Maya took a deep breath. "Aaryan, you are the love of my life. You have given me the happiest days, the most beautiful memories. I promise to love you with all my heart, today and forever."

Aaryan smiled. "That was even better."

They laughed, then practiced holding hands formally, then kissing...

And soon, the practice turned into something more. Their kisses deepened; their touches became more urgent. There was no rush, no hesitation—just pure love. They made love that night longer than usual, celebrating the fact that their dream was finally coming true. Maya whispered Aaryan's name against his skin, and he held her as if he would never let go. They loved each other until midnight, lost in the moment, lost in each other. And when they finally drifted off to sleep, they knew—this was just the beginning of forever.

*****

The morning sunlight streamed through the window of Maya's apartment, casting a soft glow over the room where Aaryan and Maya lay entangled in each other's arms. It was their last day in Kuala Lumpur before they set out for their wedding in Melaka. Today, there were no trips to take, no shopping to do—just a peaceful day spent together, cherishing every moment before their biggest adventure began.

Maya stirred first, her fingers lightly tracing the outline of Aaryan's face. "Wake up, sleepyhead," she whispered.

Aaryan groaned, pulling her closer. "Five more minutes," he mumbled.

Maya laughed softly, running her fingers through his hair. "You say that every morning but today is special. We need to get ready."

Aaryan opened one eye. "Ready for what? We're just packing today."

Maya smirked. "Yes, but don't forget, we have something even more important to do."

Aaryan stretched lazily. "And what is that?"

Maya kissed his nose. "You're going to learn how to make *nasi lemak* today."

Aaryan sat up, pretending to be shocked. "Wait, I thought I was the student. Who made you the master chef?"

Maya giggled. "I've been eating nasi lemak since childhood and cooking it for a long time, so that makes me an expert."

Aaryan winked. "Fine, teach me, *guru ji*."

Maya rolled her eyes playfully. "Follow me to the kitchen, my dear student."

The kitchen filled with the rich aroma of coconut milk, pandan leaves, and fried anchovies. Maya stood by the counter, chopping ingredients while Aaryan watched her closely.

"Okay, first step," Maya said, pointing to the rice. "We cook it with coconut milk, pandan leaves, and a pinch of salt. This gives it that creamy, fragrant taste."

Aaryan nodded seriously, pouring the ingredients into the pot. "So far, so good."

Maya smirked. "Now, we fry peanuts and anchovies."

Aaryan did as instructed, but as soon as he turned his attention back to Maya, he couldn't resist teasing her. He walked up behind her, slipping his arms around her waist. "You know," he whispered, his breath warm against her neck, "I think I'd rather taste something sweeter than this dish."

Maya rolled her eyes but leaned into his embrace. "Aaryan, focus!" she scolded playfully.

Aaryan kissed her neck softly. "I am focused. Just not on the food."

Maya giggled, trying to push him away, but he held her tighter, his hands sliding over her waist, then slowly moving up.

She swatted his hands away. "Stop distracting me! Do you want to learn it or not?"

Aaryan chuckled, stepping back. "Fine, fine. I'll behave."

Maya turned back to the stove, shaking her head with a smile. "Sometimes, I feel like I'm teaching a naughty child instead of my future husband."

Aaryan smirked. "A naughty child who loves his teacher a little too much."

They continued cooking, Aaryan following Maya's instructions carefully. She was surprised by how quickly he picked up the techniques.

"You're actually really good at this," she admitted, watching him stir the sambal sauce with precision.

Aaryan shrugged. "I cook often. I love learning new dishes."

Maya nodded, impressed. "I have to say, you're a good student, Mr. Kapoor."

Aaryan grinned. "And you're the best teacher, *Mrs. Kapoor*."

Maya paused, the words sinking in.

"Mrs. Kapoor," she repeated softly.

Aaryan gave a crooked smile. "That's what I'll call you after the wedding. No more Maya Tan. From now on, you'll be Maya Kapoor."

Maya raised an eyebrow. "Oh? Is that so?"

Aaryan nodded. "It's a tradition in India. Wives usually take their husband's surname."

Maya shrugged. "I don't mind. Call me whatever you want, just don't take your love away."

Aaryan gently held her face, looking into her eyes. "That's one thing I will never do."

Maya smiled, pressing her forehead against his. "Then I don't care what name I carry, as long as I carry your love."

That night, they enjoyed their homemade nasi lemak, laughing, talking, and savoring every bite. It wasn't just about the food—it was about the love they had poured into making it together. After dinner, they lay in bed, wrapped in each other's arms, dreaming of their upcoming wedding.

"Tomorrow, we leave for Melaka," Aaryan whispered.

Maya smiled. "Yes. The final chapter of our love story begins."

The next morning, they woke up early, filled with excitement. They packed everything they needed—their wedding outfits, their rings, and all the little things that would make their day special. By 8 AM, they were on the road. The drive from Kuala Lumpur to Melaka was only two hours, but for them, it felt like a journey toward destiny. Aaryan kept his hands on the wheel, while Maya sat beside him, brimming with enthusiasm.

"You know, Melaka is my favorite city," Maya said, gazing out the window.

Aaryan glanced at her with a smile. "Oh? Why's that?"

"I used to visit every year with my parents when I was a child," she said. "But after college and work, life got too busy. It's been seven or eight years since my last trip."

Aaryan listened intently. He had always been a man of few words, but something about Maya made him want to open up, to share more.

"You must have a lot of memories there," he said.

Maya sighed, a soft smile on her lips. "So many. And now, I get to make new ones—with you."

Aaryan reached over, taking her hand in his. "This time, I promise you won't just visit. You'll live every moment."

Maya held his hand. "That's why I love you."

They spent the entire journey talking, reminiscing, and planning.

"I'll show you every corner of Melaka," Maya said excitedly. "I'll take you to the best street food stalls, the historic sites, the riverside cafés. You'll love it!"

Aaryan chuckled. "Sounds like you have my itinerary planned already."

Maya grinned. "Of course! Melaka is the best place on Earth, and I'm going to prove it to you."

They were so lost in conversation that they didn't even realize how quickly time had passed. Before they knew it, they were entering Melaka.

Maya's eyes sparkled as she looked around. "I can't believe I'm back here after so long."

Aaryan smiled. "And this time, you're not just visiting. You're coming here to start a new chapter."

Maya nodded, tears of happiness welling up in her eyes. "Yes. And I wouldn't want it any other way."

As they drove through the streets of Melaka, the realization hit them both—their dream was finally coming true.

*****

The sun hung high in the cloudy sky as Aaryan and Maya drove into the heart of Melaka, the city that had lived in Maya's dreams for years. As they approached the grand entrance of The Majestic Hotel Melaka, Aaryan couldn't help but notice the colonial-style building, a structure that spoke of history, culture, and luxury all at once. It was a masterpiece of heritage, blending old-world charm with modern indulgence.

Maya sighed in satisfaction as she stepped out of the car. "This is it, Aaryan. The best hotel in Melaka. I wanted our stay here to be nothing short of perfect."

Aaryan curled his lips. "You sure know how to pick a place. But looking at this hotel, I think I need to check my wallet again."

Maya playfully elbowed him. "No budget talks, Mr. Kapoor. Only the best for our wedding trip."

Aaryan chuckled, shaking his head. "Fine, fine. I surrender."

They stepped inside, greeted by the scent of jasmine and polished wood. The reception area exuded grandeur—high ceilings, Peranakan-style tiles, and antique furnishings transported them to a bygone era.

"Welcome to The Majestic Hotel Melaka," the receptionist said with a warm smile. "Your suite is ready for you."

Minutes later, they entered their room—an elegant blend of colonial architecture and Malay heritage. The four-poster bed, the wooden furniture, and the large windows overlooking the Melaka River made it feel surreal. Maya twirled around in excitement.

"I can't believe we're finally here!" she exclaimed, her eyes shining.

Aaryan dropped his bags and stretched. "Well, if this is how royalty feels, I could get used to it."

Maya rolled her eyes. "You'll get used to it for five days. Then back to reality!"

Aaryan laughed. "Fair enough."

Without wasting time, Maya grabbed Aaryan's hand and pulled him outside. "Come on! I have so much to show you!"

It was almost noon, but the overcast sky made their stroll through the city pleasant. Aaryan observed everything with keen eyes—old colonial mansions, intricately designed temples, and European-inspired cafés lining the Melaka River.

He looked at Maya. "This reminds me of Penang, but Melaka feels cozier, more... humble."

Maya nodded. "Exactly! That's why I love it so much."

As they walked through the narrow streets, Maya became his personal tour guide, pointing out the historical significance of every place they passed. Aaryan listened intently, absorbing the rich culture of the city.

"Melaka was once a thriving trading port," Maya explained. "The Portuguese, the Dutch, and the British all ruled here at different times. That's why you see so many colonial-style buildings mixed with Chinese and Malay influences."

Aaryan was fascinated. "I can see why this place is special to you."

Maya smiled. "Just wait. There's more."

They soon arrived at Dutch Square, also known as the Red Square, famous for its vibrant red buildings and European-style architecture. The Christ Church, the Stadthuys, and the clock tower stood proudly, whispering tales of Melaka's colonial past.

Aaryan took out his phone. "We need some pictures here."

They took several photos, capturing the essence of the square. Suddenly, Aaryan spotted a watermelon juice stall, his face lighting up with excitement.

"Wait, watermelon juice? That's new!"

Maya chuckled. "It's common here. Why, don't you have watermelon in Delhi?"

Aaryan smirked. "Of course, we do! But we eat it as slices, not as juice."

Maya playfully pulled him across the street. "Then you have to try this!"

She ordered a large, freshly squeezed watermelon juice, served in a carved-out watermelon shell with a straw. Aaryan took a sip and sighed in relief.

"This... this is heaven," he said. "Perfect for the humidity."

Maya proudly said, "Told you. Now, let's go before you get stuck here."

Their next stop was A Famosa, the ancient Portuguese fortress that stood as a relic of Melaka's war-torn past.

Aaryan marveled at the stone walls and archways, imagining the battles fought centuries ago. "It's hard to believe this was built in the 1500s."

Maya nodded. "It was one of the strongest fortresses of its time, but the British destroyed most of it. This gateway is all that remains."

They walked through every corner, feeling the weight of history around them.

Aaryan sighed. "Places like this remind you how small we are in the grand scheme of time."

Maya took his hand. "That's why we have to live every moment to the fullest."

Aaryan kissed her forehead. "With you, I always do."

On their way back, they noticed a street artist sketching portraits for tourists.

Maya's eyes sparkled. "Aaryan, let's get one!"

Aaryan said, "Sure. But let's make it special."

Maya tilted her head. "How?"

Aaryan pulled her onto his lap. "Sketch us like this."

The artist chuckled but started working quickly. Within ten minutes, he produced a detailed, lifelike sketch of them—Maya sitting on Aaryan's lap, her arms wrapped around his neck, both smiling.

Maya was thrilled. "This is beautiful!"

Aaryan paid 30 ringgits plus a 10-ringgit tip and thanked the artist. As they walked away, Maya clutched the sketch to her chest. "This is going to our wedding album."

Aaryan smiled. "And one day, it'll be framed in our home."

Maya's heart swelled with happiness. "I can't wait."

As they made their way back to the hotel, the sun was setting over the Melaka Strait, drenching the city in a radiant, golden light.

Maya stopped for a moment, watching the view. "Look at that, Aaryan. Isn't it beautiful?"

Aaryan wrapped an arm around her waist. "Not as beautiful as you."

She smiled, resting her head on his shoulder.

As they walked through the local streets, Maya spotted a foot massage parlor.

"Aaryan, let's get a massage!" she said excitedly.

Aaryan laughed. "After all the walking today, I won't say no."

They entered the small, cozy place, where two skilled masseuses massaged their feet, relieving the fatigue of the day. Aaryan let out a satisfied sigh.

"I think I could stay here forever."

Maya said excitedly, "You'll have to, because I'm not leaving Melaka anytime soon."

That night, they dined at a South Indian restaurant, craving something familiar. They ordered dosa with sambar and chicken biryani. Aaryan took a bite and groaned in delight.

"This is amazing. I missed Indian spices!"

Maya laughed. "You're saying that after claiming you're addicted to Malaysian food?"

Aaryan said while lifting his shoulders, "What can I say? I have a big heart... and a bigger stomach."

Maya rolled her eyes. "That's why I love you."

After dinner, they walked by the Melaka River, hand in hand, before returning to their luxury hotel.

As they lay in bed, Aaryan whispered, "One day down, a few more to go. And then... we get married."

Maya smiled. "I can't wait to be Mrs. Kapoor."

With that, sleep gradually claimed them, carrying them into dreams of love, history, and the future they were about to build together.

Love, in its purest and most consuming form, has the power to eclipse everything else—pain, fear, even the cruel certainty of fate. When one is truly, madly in love, the world outside fades, its harshest realities dissolving into the background like whispers in the wind. Nothing else matters, not the past, not the future—only the heartbeat of the one they adore. Maya, standing on the edge of time, should have been drowning in the weight of her fate. Yet, in Aaryan's arms, love was stronger than time, stronger than death itself.

*****

The pleasant morning sunlight filtered through the expansive windows of The Majestic Hotel Melaka, enveloping the opulent interiors in warm, caramel radiance. Saturday had arrived, marking the last weekend before their wedding. Maya and Aaryan walked hand in hand into the hotel's grand restaurant, only to freeze in amazement.

Aaryan let out a low whistle. "Are we in a five-star hotel or a royal banquet?"

Maya's eyes danced with excitement as she scanned the extravagant breakfast buffet. There were hundreds of dishes from more than ten different cuisines. Every possible breakfast item—from fresh-baked pastries, local Malaysian delicacies, Indian parathas, Western-style omelets, and tropical fruits—was arranged in perfection.

"This is insane," Maya breathed.

Aaryan chuckled. "You wanted the best experience in Melaka? Here it is."

They loaded their plates with everything they could handle—nasi lemak with spicy sambal, dim sum baskets, buttery croissants, mango sticky rice, a fluffy cheese omelet, fresh watermelon juice, and a cup of perfectly brewed coffee.

By the time they were done, Aaryan leaned back, rubbing his stomach. "I think I need to be rolled out of here."

Maya giggled, patting his arm. "Good. We'll need all the energy for later."

Aaryan raised an eyebrow. "What do you mean?"

Maya winked. "Just wait and see."

As soon as they stepped outside, a wave of heat hit them. The sun was ruthless, and the air was thick with humidity.

"God, it's boiling," Aaryan groaned.

"Which is why," Maya said smugly, "we're spending the afternoon in the hotel pool."

They changed into their swimwear and headed to the infinity pool overlooking the city. The water was a cool, crystal-blue oasis that seemed to stretch into the horizon.

Aaryan hesitated at the pool's edge. "You know I can't swim, right?"

Maya rolled her eyes. "We're not swimming. We're just sitting here, cooling off."

They settled into the shallow end, their bodies half-submerged, as they ordered a pineapple juice packed with ice.

Aaryan took a long sip, sighing in satisfaction. "This is pure bliss."

Maya smiled. "Let's talk about the wedding."

Maya looked at Aaryan, a soft smile playing on her lips. "Do you remember why I chose 6th April?"

Aaryan frowned, thinking hard. "I can't remember."

Maya's smile faded slightly. "You forgot? We finished college on 6th April and didn't meet after that... until this trip of yours."

Aaryan's eyes lit up as realization struck. "Oh yes! I remember now. That's why you chose 6th April?"

Maya nodded, her fingers tracing the water's surface.

For a moment, they sat in silence, absorbing the weight of their decision.

Then Maya suddenly brightened. "Oh! Jonker Walk is tonight!"

Aaryan groaned. "Another walk? I think I had enough of that yesterday."

Maya burst out laughing. "It's not a walk-walk. It's a night market! You have never seen anything like that.

Aaryan eyed her skeptically. "What's so special about it?"

Maya impatiently said, "You'll see."

As the sun dipped below the horizon, Jonker Walk came alive. The famous weekend night market, stretching along Jalan Hang Jebat, was a spectacle of colors, lights, and the rich aroma of street food. Aaryan's eyes grew wide at the rows of stalls selling everything from handmade crafts, antiques, souvenirs, clothes, jewelry, and street performances.

"This... is madness," he muttered.

Maya laughed, pulling him forward. "This is Melaka's heart."

They moved through the bustling crowd, stopping at various stalls. Aaryan spotted a vendor making crispy spring rolls at lightning speed.

"What's this?" he asked.

"Popiah," Maya said. "A Malaysian-style fresh spring roll. Try it."

Aaryan took a bite, and his expressions lit up with surprise. "Holy—this is delicious!"

Maya smirked. "Told you."

They also tried coconut ice cream served in a coconut shell, grilled satay skewers, and peanut pancakes called Apam Balik. As they walked, they passed a man playing a traditional Chinese instrument, the erhu, his melancholic tune filling the night air. Aaryan stopped to listen.

Maya touched his arm. "Music here tells stories. Just like Melaka itself."

Aaryan nodded. He was beginning to fall in love with this city.

They picked up a couple of souvenirs—a hand-painted batik scarf for Maya and a keychain shaped like Melaka's A Famosa fort for Aaryan.

After hours of exploring, they settled at a small, rustic café on the corner—Café Geographer.

"This place is famous for travelers," Maya said as they found a cozy corner table. "It's a mix of history, great food, and a place where strangers become friends."

Aaryan picked up the menu. "What's good here?"

Maya beamed with joy. "Try the chicken sandwich, pizza, and salad. And... maybe you should learn about Baba-Nyonya culture while you're at it."

Aaryan raised an eyebrow. "Baba-Nyonya?"

Maya leaned forward. "The Peranakans. They are descendants of Chinese immigrants who settled in Malacca, Penang, and Singapore centuries ago. Over time, they blended Chinese and Malay culture, creating their own language, traditions, and even cuisine."

Aaryan listened intently. "So, their food is...?"

"A mix of Chinese ingredients with Malay spices. That's why Nyonya food is so special."

Aaryan smirked. "Why didn't you tell me all this earlier?"

Maya laughed. "Because I wanted to see your reaction."

They enjoyed a delicious meal at Café Geographer and quickly drifted off to sleep.

Sunday morning arrived, but something felt different. The distant hum of the city and the gentle rustling of palm trees added to the morning's serenity. Yet, beneath it all, an unusual stillness lingered.

Maya was quiet.

Aaryan noticed—he always did. But he didn't press her. Instead, he watched as she absently stirred her coffee, her gaze fixed on some distant point beyond the window. He could feel the weight of her thoughts, the unspoken heaviness in her silence.

After breakfast, they made their way to the poolside, choosing a secluded spot where the sound of water lapping against the pool's edge and the occasional laughter of children playing filled the air. Aaryan stretched out on a lounge chair, his sunglasses perched on his nose, while Maya sat beside him, her arms wrapped around her knees.

The afternoon stretched lazily before them, and instead of venturing outside, they chose to stay in, exploring the amenities of their luxurious hotel. They wandered through the grand hallways, visited the spa where Maya let the soothing scent of lavender and chamomile calm her senses, and later, they took a quiet swim in the infinity pool, floating side by side in silence. Every now and then, Aaryan would glance at her, but Maya's thoughts remained locked away, far beyond his reach.

The weight in her heart wasn't something she could put into words. For the first time in weeks, she wasn't afraid of dying. Instead, she was afraid of leaving behind happiness. She was afraid of what Aaryan would feel when she was no longer here.

By the time evening arrived, something in Maya shifted. The heaviness wasn't gone, but there was a lightness in her steps. She turned to Aaryan with a small smile and said, "Let's go for a walk."

Aaryan looked at her, studying her face. There was something different in her eyes—a kind of quiet acceptance. He nodded. "Along the Malacca River?"

She nodded. "Yes. I feel like walking there."

The streets of Malacca were alive with the soft glow of lanterns and the distant murmur of conversations. They strolled hand in hand along the river, the water reflecting the twinkling lights of the city. Small boats cruised gently, their passengers laughing and taking pictures. The riverside restaurants were bustling, the aroma of grilled food and spices filling the air. Tourists walked past them, some pausing to admire the intricate decorations along the promenade.

Yet, between Aaryan and Maya, words were few. They didn't need them. Every step, every glance, every squeeze of their intertwined fingers spoke volumes. They walked for an hour, taking in the sights and sounds, pausing now and then to watch a street performer or to admire the intricate murals along the walls of old buildings. The river shimmered under the moonlight, and a gentle breeze played with Maya's hair.

Aaryan suddenly stopped, his eyes falling on the familiar sight of Café Geographer. He liked the meal they had here the night before so much that he wanted to eat there again.

"Maya," he said, turning to her. "What do you say we have dinner here again?"

She followed his gaze and smiled softly. "You really liked it, huh?"

"I did," he admitted. "And it just feels... right to come back here tonight."

Maya nodded. "Then let's do it."

They stepped inside, the warm, inviting ambiance of the café wrapping around them like a familiar embrace. The wooden interiors, the lively yet soothing jazz music playing in the background, and the comforting aroma of delicious food made it feel like a perfect choice for their last dinner before the big day.

They ordered the same dishes as before, except this time, instead of a salad, they added dim sum to their meal. As they waited, Aaryan reached across the table, taking Maya's hand in his. His thumb traced slow, reassuring circles on her palm.

She met his gaze. "What?" she asked softly.

"Just... making sure you're here," he said.

Her heart clenched. "I'm here, Aaryan."

Their food arrived, and they ate in comfortable silence. The dim sum was soft, flavorful, and comforting, each bite melting in their mouths. Aaryan relished every flavor, knowing he would forever associate this meal with this very moment.

After dinner, they stepped out into the night, walking back toward the hotel. The air was cooler now, the city quieter as the night deepened. Their hands remained clasped, fingers fitting together effortlessly.

As they reached their hotel, they lingered at the entrance for a moment. Maya glanced up at Aaryan, her eyes reflecting something deep, something unspoken.

"Tomorrow," she whispered.

Aaryan smiled, brushing a strand of hair from her face. "Tomorrow."

They walked into the hotel and made their way to their room. The exhaustion of the day, both physical and emotional, settled in as they changed into their nightclothes. They climbed into bed, lying close, their foreheads almost touching.

Aaryan exhaled. "You, okay?"

Maya nodded. "Are you?"

He paused. "I will be."

Silence stretched between them again, but it wasn't empty. It was filled with everything they felt but didn't say. Tomorrow was their wedding, and deep down, they both knew they were running out of time. Aaryan reached for Maya's hand under the blanket, giving it a gentle embrace. She squeezed back. No words were needed. Moments like these don't last forever. But tonight, they held onto them anyway. Sleep came quickly, pulling them both into a world of dreams, a world where time didn't matter, where love existed beyond the limits of days and nights. Tomorrow was a big day, and they were ready to face it together.

*****

The sun rose slowly over Melaka, it was a new day, a special day, yet a strangely quiet one. Maya and Aaryan stood at the entrance of the wedding venue, fingers entwined. It was a heritage bungalow-turned-hotel, surrounded by lush green gardens, a place Maya had chosen long ago for her wedding. There were no guests. No friends. No family. Just the two of them... and the wedding officiator, a retired government officer, formally dressed in a beige suit. Aaryan adjusted his grey suit, looking at Maya. She was breathtaking. Her snow-white gown flowed behind her, the delicate lace hugging her frame, her dark hair pinned up elegantly with soft curls cascading down her back.

Maya smiled softly. “Ready?”

Aaryan exhaled. “I was ready the moment I saw you in college.”

Maya chuckled. “Cheesy.”

“You like it,” Aaryan smirked.

The officiator cleared his throat, gesturing for them to step forward. The ceremony was short, simple, and intimate. Maya had arranged for the rituals to be done as per her culture, while Aaryan, being a non-believer, didn’t mind not having Hindu customs.

As they exchanged rings, Aaryan held Maya’s hand firmly, looking into her eyes. “I love you more than anyone in this world,” he said, his voice raw with emotion.

Maya’s lips trembled, her eyes shining with unshed tears. She leaned in, pressing a soft, lingering kiss against his lips.

"Love you too," she whispered.

There was no grand applause. No cheering crowd. Just them. And yet, at that moment, it felt like the world had paused in reverence for their love. After the ceremony, they were seated at a large traditional banquet table, with elegant chairs that looked like they belonged to a royal palace. Aaryan looked around, surprised at the detailed arrangements. The table was adorned with candles, flowers, and fine porcelain plates.

"Maya... you planned all this?"

Maya smiled proudly. "Of course. Just because it's just us, doesn't mean it shouldn't be perfect."

Waiters soon arrived, serving small portions of Indian and Malay cuisines. They started with chicken satay with peanut sauce, then moved on to butter chicken, nasi lemak, biryani, and freshly baked naan. The flavors exploded in their mouths, a beautiful blend of spice and richness.

Aaryan picked up a bite of nasi lemak, feeding it to Maya. "For my beautiful bride."

Maya laughed, taking the bite. "Mmm... delicious."

She picked up a spoonful of *gulab jamun* (an Indian sweet) and held it to Aaryan's lips. "Your turn."

Aaryan groaned as he tasted the sweet syrupy dessert. "Damn, this is good."

They continued feeding each other, giggling, drinking wine, and talking nonsense—just like two people who had forgotten the world outside. Three hours passed before they finally decided to leave. As they walked out, hand in hand, husband and wife, Aaryan whispered, "Thank you for making this perfect."

Maya pinched his fingers. "It was perfect because you were in it."

Back in their hotel room, they changed into comfortable nightwear and sat on the bed, talking endlessly about their college days.

"Remember Raj?" Aaryan laughed. "That guy who failed every subject except *beer drinking?*"

Maya burst out laughing. "Oh my God, yes! He used to copy from my assignments and still fail!"

Aaryan laughed out loud. "And remember how you used to ignore me for weeks?"

Maya raised an eyebrow. "You deserved it."

They kept talking until the conversation faded into silence.

Maya looked at Aaryan, her fingers tracing the buttons of his shirt. "We're married now."

Aaryan's eyes softened. "Yes."

Her voice dropped to a whisper. "Then let's love each other like there's no tomorrow."

There was something in her tone that sent a shiver down his spine. She meant it literally. He cupped her face, kissing her deeply, his hands slowly roaming down her body. Their kisses were needy, desperate, yet filled with love. That night, they made love for hours, exploring each other with the tenderness of lovers who knew their time was limited. There was no rush. No distractions. Only them. And the soft glow of candlelight illuminating their tangled bodies.

Long after their passion had settled into soft whispers and lingering touches, they lay entwined beneath the sheets, their breaths steadying in unison. Aaryan traced slow, absentminded circles on Maya's bare back, his fingers memorizing the warmth of her skin.

Maya nestled closer, resting her head against his chest, listening to the rhythmic beating of his heart. "I wish this night could last forever," she murmured sleepily.

Aaryan kissed the top of her head. "It already does," he whispered.

The candlelight flickered as the night deepened, wrapping them in its quiet embrace. Eventually, exhaustion took over, and they drifted into sleep, holding onto each other as if letting go would mean losing everything.

The next morning, they packed their bags and checked out of the hotel. Maya was weaker than usual. Her skin looked paler, her movements slower.

Aaryan frowned as he held her hand in the car. "You're looking weak, Maya."

She smiled faintly. "It's just tiredness."

Aaryan squeezed her fingers. "Don't worry, I'll take care of you. I'll make you healthy again."

Maya looked out of the window, her heart aching. She knew that wasn't possible.

She wasn't taking her medications, the ones that could have prolonged her life for a few more months. She had already given up on them a week ago, a decision she made silently, without telling Aaryan. She didn't want to drag on her suffering. More importantly, she didn't want Aaryan to suffer. She would rather leave him sooner than watch him care for a dying woman, than see the love in his eyes slowly turn into helplessness. So, she kept her secret, carrying the weight of it alone, knowing that every passing day was bringing her closer to the inevitable.

As they drove through the highways of Malaysia, the city skyline of Kuala Lumpur appeared in the distance.

Maya took a deep breath. "Aaryan, I need you to promise me something."

Aaryan didn't respond. He just kept holding her hand, his grip tightening.

Maya continued, her voice steady. "Promise me that after I'm gone... you'll marry someone again."

Aaryan clenched his jaw.

Maya's eyes filled with tears. "Promise me you'll move on and live your life to the fullest."

Aaryan kept his face emotionless, but inside, he was screaming. He simply nodded and kissed her hand. Maya understood—sometimes, silence carried more pain than words ever could.

By the time they reached their apartment, Maya could barely stand. After a light dinner, they sat on the balcony, watching the city lights. Then, suddenly, Maya clutched her stomach. Her body tensed.

Aaryan rushed to her side. "Maya?"

She ran to the bathroom and vomited violently.

Aaryan held her hair, rubbing her back. "It's okay, it's okay."

But she vomited again... and again.

Her body trembled. Pain gripped her stomach. Her head throbbed. Aaryan never left her side. He sat beside her all night, letting her rest her head in his lap. Gently, he massaged her temples and rubbed her back, offering what little comfort he could.

Maya gripped his hand weakly. "Aaryan..."

He pressed his lips to her forehead. "I'm here, Maya."

She closed her eyes, exhausted, and slowly drifted into sleep, her head resting quietly on Aaryan's lap. He watched her, his fingers gently running through her hair, memorizing every slow, shallow breath she took.

That night, he didn't sleep. He just held her. And prayed to a God he didn't believe in... to let her stay a little longer.

*****

Aaryan opened his eyes to the dimly lit room, the curtains barely letting in the gentle radiance of the sunrise. His body ached with exhaustion, but his arms were still wrapped around Maya, who was fast asleep beside him. The night had been long. He had stayed up massaging her forehead, and stroking her back, trying to ease her pain. Every time she moaned in discomfort, he whispered reassurances into her ear, though he wasn't sure if she heard them.

Maya stirred slightly and let out a soft sigh. Aaryan tightened his hold on her.

"You need to rest, love," Maya murmured, her voice hoarse.

Aaryan kissed the top of her head. "I will, but only if you promise to rest too."

Maya nodded weakly. "I don't have the energy to do anything else."

She tried to sit up, but her body refused to cooperate. Aaryan quickly helped her, adjusting the pillows behind her back.

"Water?" he asked, already reaching for the glass.

She nodded. He brought the glass to her lips, watching as she took slow, measured sips. After a few seconds, she handed it back and sighed.

"I need to use the bathroom."

Aaryan helped her up, guiding her slowly towards the washroom. It took effort, but she managed. When she came back, she looked exhausted again. Without a word, she climbed into bed beside him and snuggled into his chest.

Aaryan smiled softly. This was rare. Maya had never been someone who clung to him for comfort. She was independent, strong-willed. But now, in her fragile state, she held onto him as though he was the only thing keeping her alive. And maybe, in some ways, he was. As they drifted back into sleep, Aaryan silently prayed that she would wake up stronger.

They woke up in the afternoon. Aaryan stretched, feeling much better after the rest. But when he turned to Maya, he saw the same tiredness in her eyes.

"You're still weak," he observed, placing a hand on her forehead. "No fever, but you look exhausted."

Maya smiled faintly. "I'm fine. Just need some time."

Aaryan sighed. "You still owe me a proper tour of Kuala Lumpur, you know? We've traveled to Langkawi, Penang, Melaka, and Cameron Highlands, but we never explored this city together."

Maya nodded slowly. "Yes, I know. I've lived in Kuala Lumpur all my life, and I love this city more than anything." She exhaled heavily. "We'll see places when I get stronger."

Aaryan stroked her cheek. "Take all the time you need. I just want you to get better first."

Maya didn't respond. She knew that wouldn't happen.

The next seven days were a test of love and endurance. Maya's health didn't improve. She remained weak, tired, and in pain. Aaryan dedicated himself completely to her.

He cooked for her every day—simple soups, nasi lemak (her favorite), and anything else she could manage to eat. He ordered food when needed, carefully selecting meals that wouldn't upset her fragile body.

He cleaned the apartment, washed and ironed clothes, massaged her for hours—especially when her headaches became unbearable. And through it all, he never complained. There was no frustration in his voice, no exhaustion in his touch. He did it all because he loved her.

There was no physical intimacy between them during these days. Maya was too weak, too drained. But their love didn't need words or touches. It was in the way Aaryan carried her when she couldn't walk, in the way he kissed her forehead every night, in the way he whispered 'I love you' when he thought she was asleep.

Maya often watched him, her heart aching. How could anyone love someone so much? She was dying. Yet, he treated her like she was his whole world. One afternoon, Fatimah came to visit.

Maya smiled weakly when she saw her. "You look beautiful."

Fatimah sat beside her, taking her hand. "You look terrible."

Maya chuckled softly. "I know."

Aaryan greeted Fatimah politely and excused himself to make tea. As they sat together, Maya couldn't stop talking about Aaryan.

"He does everything for me, Fatimah. He feeds me, bathes me, massages me when my body aches. I don't even have to ask—he just knows what I need."

Fatimah smiled. "You're lucky to have him."

Maya sighed. "I know. I'm super lucky."

Fatimah placed a hand on hers. "Then fight, Maya. Live for him."

Maya didn't reply. She just smiled sadly. She wasn't fighting. She was simply waiting for the end.

Later that day, the call came—the one that shattered Aaryan's world. His father was gone. The phone felt heavy in his hand; his fingers numb as he gripped it. A wave of disbelief washed over him, his breath hitching. His vision blurred, and for a moment, the world around him faded. He turned to Maya, his voice breaking, struggling to form the words that would make it real.

"Papa is gone."

Maya's heart clenched. She reached for him, pulling him into an embrace. Aaryan broke down, sobbing into her shoulder.

Maya stroked his hair, whispering, "Go, Aaryan. Be with your family."

He shook his head violently. "I can't leave you. Not like this."

Maya cradled his face. "You must. Who's gone is gone. But I am still here, Aaryan. Go, be with your family. Come back in a few days."

Aaryan refused. "I can't leave you. You're weak. You need me."

Maya pleaded. “Fatimah can stay with me. Please, Aaryan.”

After much persuasion, Aaryan reluctantly agreed, though every fiber of his being resisted the idea of leaving Maya, even for a moment. He hesitated, searching her face for any sign of discomfort, but Maya gave him a reassuring smile, holding his hand softly.

Still unsure, he finally picked up the phone and called Fatimah. Without hesitation, she promised to come right away, assuring Aaryan that she would stay with Maya and take care of her. “Don’t worry,” Fatimah said gently. “She’ll be in safe hands.”

Even as the call ended, Aaryan lingered by Maya’s side, sweeping a loose strand from her face. “Are you sure about this?” he asked one last time.

Maya nodded. “Go, Aaryan. Just for a little while. I’ll be fine.”

With a reluctant sigh, he pressed a kiss on her forehead, silently hoping that stepping away, even briefly, wouldn’t mean losing another moment with her.

Aaryan booked a flight to Delhi for the next morning. Worried and anxious about leaving Maya in this state, he couldn't sleep all night. He spent the night by her side, holding her in his arms, caressing her, watching her as if trying to memorize every detail. He wasn’t ready to leave, but attending his father’s last rituals was crucial. He reassured himself that Maya’s weakness was just exhaustion from their recent travels. What he didn’t know was that she hadn’t been taking her medicines.

The next morning, as Aaryan was preparing to leave, he took extra time explaining everything to Fatimah.

"This is where the food is... This is the medicine she refuses to take... This is her favorite blanket... She gets cold at night, so make sure—"

Maya just watched him, tears in her eyes. How could anyone love her this much?

Aaryan turned to her. His flight was in a couple of hours. He hugged her and didn't let go for two full minutes. Then, he kissed her forehead, her cheeks, and finally her lips.

"I'll be back in five days," he promised. "And we'll make your last days unforgettable."

Maya smiled, hiding her pain. Tears welled in Fatimah's eyes as Aaryan picked up his bag and left.

Aaryan's flight landed in Delhi just after midnight. The air was warm, the city was unusually quiet at this hour. He stepped out of the airport, dragging his small suitcase behind him, but his heart felt heavier than his luggage.

He hailed a taxi and sat silently in the backseat, staring blankly at the passing streets. His father was gone. The reality hadn't sunk in yet. He had spent years away from home, years of strained relationships and disagreements, and now, just like that, his father was no more. But his grief was divided. His father was dead, but Maya was dying.

The moment he stepped into his house, the atmosphere was suffocating. The lights were dimmed, and the entire place was filled with relatives, their voices murmuring in hushed tones. His mother sat in a corner, her *saree* draped loosely over her frail shoulders, her eyes swollen from endless crying.

Aaryan's breath hitched his throat. His mother had lost her husband. He had lost his father. As soon as he approached, his mother looked up. For a moment, she just stared at him, and then she broke down completely. But before rushing to her, Aaryan turned to his father's lifeless body, his heart clenching at the sight. He knelt beside him, his fingers trembling as he touched his father's cold hand. He whispered a silent goodbye, his eyes stinging with unshed tears. With a deep breath, he folded his hands in prayer, paying his last respects to the man who had raised him.

Then, as his mother's quiet sobs filled the room, he stood up and rushed to her side, pulling her into a tight embrace. She clung to him like she had been holding in her pain, waiting for him to arrive.

"Aaryan... your father..." she choked out, unable to say more.

Aaryan's own tears fell freely as he whispered, "I know, Maa... I know..."

They sat there for what felt like an eternity, grieving together. The weight of the past, the unresolved arguments, the years of distance, it all crushed him in that moment.

For the next four days, Aaryan went through his grief like a lifeless shadow, empty and lost. He participated in the rituals, met relatives, accepted condolences, and listened to people say things like, "He lived a good life" or "He's in a better place now." But inside, he felt completely disconnected.

His father's death should have consumed him. It should have been the only thing on his mind. But it wasn't. Because every second, his mind was in Malaysia. With Maya.

Every hour, he picked up his phone and called her.

“Maya, how are you? Are you taking your medicines? Is Fatimah taking care of you? Are you eating properly?” Aaryan asked, his voice laced with desperation.

“I'm fine, Aaryan,” she said, forcing brightness into her voice. “Fatimah is taking care of me. Don't worry about me. How's your mother?”

“She's...” He hesitated. “She's trying to stay strong.”

“Then you should stay strong too,” Maya said softly. “For her. For yourself.”

Aaryan swallowed hard. “I just... I wish I could be there with you.”

“I'm waiting for you,” she whispered.

Her words made his chest tighten. He knew she wasn't well—her voice, was too soft, too fragile. But she never admitted it. She was lying to protect him.

Still, he clung to hope, convincing himself that Maya had more time—that she would hold on for at least three or four more months. That they still had precious days left. That if he returned quickly enough, everything would be okay again.

Aaryan barely slept that night. He lay in his childhood bed, staring at the ceiling, his mind racing with a thousand thoughts. Images of his father's lifeless body flashed in his mind. But so did images of Maya, without him in that apartment, growing weaker with every passing second.

He could almost hear her voice—soft, tired, struggling to breathe. He turned onto his side, squeezing his eyes shut. She's okay. She's okay. But deep down, he knew she wasn't.

His mother barely spoke to him about Maya. She acknowledged nothing. She had known about their wedding. She had known about Maya's illness. But for her, Maya was already dead.

She didn't ask how Maya was doing. She didn't ask about his life in Malaysia. She didn't ask when he would go back. It was as if Maya didn't exist in her world.

Aaryan wanted to bring it up. He wanted to tell his mother about how much he loved Maya, about how she was all he could think about. But every time he opened his mouth, the words died on his tongue. Because he knew what his mother would say.

"She's going to die, Aaryan. Move on." But he couldn't. He wouldn't.

*****

Aaryan sat at the boarding gate, his hands gripping the armrests of the chair. His mind had been restless for the last five days, but now, as he waited for his flight to Kuala Lumpur, the anxiety in his chest felt unbearable. His father's death had left a hole in his heart, but the fear of losing Maya was something else entirely.

The announcement echoed through the airport: "Passengers traveling to Kuala Lumpur, your boarding is now open."

Aaryan's heart pounded. His fingers trembled as he reached for his phone, needing to see her—just for a moment.

For the past five days, he had spoken to her endlessly—15 to 20 times a day—but each call had lasted less than a minute. Caught up in performing his father's last rituals, attending to relatives, and fulfilling his duties as a son, he had barely found time to breathe. Video calls never happened—not just because Maya always found an excuse, but because he had been too occupied to insist.

His fingers hovered over the screen. He called. The phone rang. And then—she picked up.

The moment Maya's face appeared on the screen; his heart sank. Her face was pale—unnaturally pale. Her cheeks had hollowed, her lips dry and cracked. Her once bright, expressive eyes looked sunken and weak.

"Maya..." His voice broke.

She tried to smile but barely had strength.

Aaryan swallowed the lump in his throat. "You were lying to me," he whispered. "That's why you didn't pick up my video calls, right? You didn't want me to see you like this."

Maya's lips parted, as if she wanted to deny it, but her silence was enough.

Aaryan's breath quickened. "Maya, I would have come earlier. Why did you do this? Why didn't you tell me?"

She struggled to speak; her voice was nothing more than a whisper. "Aaryan... don't worry... I'm fine."

He shook his head viciously. "You're not fine, Maya! You look so sick. Is Fatimah taking care of you properly? Why are you so weak?"

Maya coughed slightly and whispered, "I can't wait to see you."

Tears streamed down Aaryan's face. He wiped them with his sleeve, but they wouldn't stop. His body shook as he whispered, "I love you, Maya. I love you. Please hold on, I'm coming. Just wait for me."

Maya smiled weakly, but tears glistened in her eyes. "I love you too, Aaryan."

Just then, the final boarding call echoed through the speakers. Aaryan had to go.

"Goodbye kiss," she whispered, pressing her lips to the screen.

Aaryan did the same. "I'm coming, Maya. Just hold on."

With that, the call ended. Aaryan rushed to the boarding gate, his heart pounding, his mind consumed by an unshakable fear. Something felt off, a gnawing unease he couldn't ignore. But he forced the thought aside. She would hold on. She had to.

Aaryan sank into his seat, but the tears wouldn't stop. His mind was flooded with images of Maya—weak, fragile, struggling for every breath. Her voice echoed in his head. *"I love you, Aaryan."* His fingers clenched into fists as he shut his eyes, desperate to quiet the storm raging inside him. Time stretched unbearably. The food, the announcements, the murmurs of other passengers, none of it mattered. There was only Maya.

Back in Kuala Lumpur, Fatimah panicked. Maya had barely been able to hold her glass of water. Her hands were trembling, her breathing had become irregular. Then, suddenly, she collapsed.

Fatimah screamed. "Maya! Maya, wake up!"

She pressed her fingers to Maya's wrist. Her pulse was faint. Panicked, Fatimah immediately called for an ambulance, her voice trembling as she gave the details. The operator assured her that help was on the way, but every second felt agonizingly slow.

As she waited, she grabbed her phone and frantically called Aaryan. Again. And again. And again. But his phone was unreachable. Her heart pounded as she glanced at Maya, lying motionless, her breaths shallow and weak.

Realizing Aaryan might return to an empty house with no idea where they had gone, Fatimah rushed to find a pen and paper. With shaking hands, she scribbled a note, explaining everything, and pasted it on the main door.

Just then, the wail of sirens shattered the silence. Paramedics rushed in, wasting no time as they carefully lifted Maya into the ambulance. Fatimah climbed in beside her, clutching her cold hand and whispering prayers as they sped through the city.

Hours later, Aaryan's plane touched down. The moment he switched on his phone, it buzzed relentlessly with missed calls from Fatimah. A sense of dread coiled in his chest. His fingers trembled as he dialed her back.

The moment she picked up, her voice was urgent, laced with worry. "Aaryan... Maya's not well. She's in the hospital."

His breath caught. "Which hospital?"

She hurriedly gave him the address, but before she could say another word, he was already moving.

Pulse racing, Aaryan tore through the airport, flagged down a taxi, and gave the driver the hospital's name. "As fast as you can," he urged, his voice strained with desperation.

As the city blurred past the windows, he gripped his phone tightly, praying for Maya's health. Aaryan burst through the hospital doors, his heart beating heavily.

"Where is she?" he gasped, his voice trembling. "Maya. Maya Tan."

The receptionist looked at him with sorrow in her eyes. She didn't say anything, just pointed down the hall. He ran. When he reached the ICU, his steps faltered. Fatimah was there, her husband beside her. She was crying. The moment she saw Aaryan, her sobs grew louder. She walked up to him, gripping his hands. Her lips trembled as she whispered,

"Maya's dead."

The world collapsed. Aaryan fell to his knees. His head hit the cold hospital floor. And then—he screamed. A sound of pure, broken agony. Tears poured down his face as he gasped for breath, his body convulsing with sobs.

"No... no, no, NO!" His voice cracked as he shook his head violently. "She was waiting for me. She said she was fine. I was coming back! She was waiting!"

Fatimah and her husband lifted him, guided him to a bench. But he barely felt them. His whole world had ended.

A doctor approached them. "You can see her," the doctor said gently. "Before we... wrap the body."

Aaryan nodded weakly. His legs felt like stone as he forced himself to walk toward the ICU. When he reached her, his mind screamed in denial. Maya lay there, still. Peaceful. As if merely asleep. Aaryan reached out, his fingers grazing her skin—it was cold. A hollow ache spread through his chest, tightening around his ribs like a vice. He swallowed hard, his voice barely a whisper. "Maya..." But there was no response. Only silence—heavy, unbearable.

He had so much left to do with her. They were supposed to roam Kuala Lumpur, hand in hand, discovering new streets and making new memories. They were supposed to try new places to eat, laugh over food, argue about what to order, and share every bite. She was supposed to live a little longer. Just a little longer.

His fingers trembled as he leaned down, pressing a soft kiss on her lips—a last kiss, lingering with everything he never got to say. His arms wrapped around her, pulling her close as if, for a fleeting second, he could bring her back—a last hug. His eyes searched hers, desperate for warmth, for movement, for life—but there was nothing. Just the stillness of goodbye. A last stare.

And then, the doctor's voice shattered the silence.

"We need to prepare the body for transfer immediately."

Aaryan's breath hitched. He wasn't ready. He would never be ready.

He closed his eyes, pressing his lips against her forehead, and whispered, "I love you, Maya." His voice broke on the last word.

Then, with every ounce of strength left in him, he forced himself to stand. His feet felt heavy, his heart even heavier, but he turned away and walked toward the door. With every step, it felt as if he was leaving behind a part of his soul. Because he was.

*****

The air was heavy with the scent of burning incense as Aaryan stood silently in the cremation hall, his eyes fixed on the wooden coffin where Maya lay. The hall was dimly lit, its solemn atmosphere thick with grief. Fatimah and her husband stood beside him, their faces somber, their eyes swollen from crying. Aaryan had never imagined this moment. Maya—his Maya—was lying inside that coffin, ready to be engulfed by the flames.

A Chinese monk stood at the head of the coffin, chanting in a soft, rhythmic tone, performing the final rites in the traditional manner. The low hum of prayers echoed in the silence, a sacred farewell to a soul that had touched so many lives. Aaryan didn't understand the words, but he didn't need to. His heart understood everything.

Fatimah stepped forward first, placing a single white lily on the coffin. Her lips trembled as she whispered, "Goodbye, my dear friend."

Her husband followed, bowing his head in deep respect. And then, it was Aaryan's turn. His feet felt leaden as he stepped forward. His hands shivered as he placed his palm flat on the coffin's polished surface. It was cold—lifeless—just like the body inside. A sob tore through his throat. His lips quivered, but words refused to come. What could he say? Nothing he said would bring her back.

After a long silence, he whispered, "I love you, Maya. I always will."

The coffin was then lowered into the crematorium chamber. The moment the wooden box began moving,

Aaryan felt his entire world shift. His breath caught in his throat. His feet refused to move. It was as if someone was pulling him back. He couldn't step forward, couldn't walk away. His legs trembled. The energy drained from his body. Maya was leaving. The flames flickered inside the chamber, their orange glow illuminating his tear-streaked face. Aaryan felt his soul burn with them. A part of him was turning to ashes today. And when the coffin finally disappeared behind the heavy steel doors, he felt a hollow emptiness inside him. It was over. Maya was gone.

The next morning, Aaryan held the brass urn in his hands. It was heavier than he had expected. He ran his fingers over the smooth surface, knowing that inside were the remains of the woman he had loved more than anything in this world. He packed it carefully in his bag, treating it like something sacred. And then, without looking back, he boarded a flight to India. Malaysia had once been a place of happiness, laughter, and love. It had been their dreamland, their escape.

But now, every street, every corner, every dish he once loved, everything felt empty without Maya. He could no longer bear the thought of staying. The air itself felt suffocating.

As the plane soared into the sky, leaving Kuala Lumpur behind, Aaryan stared out of the window, his vision blurred by unshed tears. All he could see was Maya.

Back in India, Aaryan placed the urn in his room, on a small table by the window. He would often stand in front of it and talk to Maya.

At night, he whispered to her.

"Maya, I saw a couple today that reminded me of us."

"Maya, I cooked your favorite noodles today. But it didn't taste the same without you."

"Maya, do you think I'll ever stop missing you?"

The urn became his last connection to her. Days turned into weeks. Weeks into months. Life moved forward—but Aaryan didn't. His mother begged him to move on, to get married, to start fresh. But every time she brought it up, he shook his head. How could he? How could he give his heart to someone else when Maya still owned every broken piece of it?

The first time Aaryan returned to Malaysia after Maya's death, it was a test of his own strength. For a year, he had avoided stepping foot in the country that had once been a second home to him. The thought of walking those streets alone, eating at the places they once dreamed of trying together, and breathing the same air without her beside him was unbearable.

But on the first anniversary of her passing, something inside him shifted. He felt an undeniable pull, as if Malaysia itself was calling him back. So, with a heart heavy yet determined, he booked his flight and made the journey. When he landed in Kuala Lumpur, a scary stillness settled over him. Everything looked the same, yet everything felt different. The vibrant city, which once pulsed with energy and adventure, now felt like a museum of his memories.

But as he walked through the streets—alone yet surrounded by echoes of the past—he realized something unexpected. Maya was still here. Not in body, but in everything else. She was in the soft laughter of couples strolling hand in hand. She was in the scent of the food stalls they had planned to visit together. She was in the skyline that she had admired, saying, *"Aaryan, look at that! It's breathtaking!"*

And for the first time in a year, Aaryan felt something other than pain. It wasn't happiness—not yet—but a strange kind of peace. From that moment, Aaryan knew—this would not be his last visit. That first trip after Maya's passing changed everything. From that year onward, every single year on Maya's death anniversary, Aaryan returned to Malaysia.

It was no longer just a visit. It was a ritual. A pilgrimage of love. Each year, he ventured beyond Kuala Lumpur, discovering parts of Malaysia they had once explored together, Penang, Langkawi, Cameron Highlands, Sabah, and even new places. But he visited Malacca on every trip, religiously.

With every journey, he felt closer to Maya. At first, the trips were filled with grief. He walked through the cities with teary eyes, retracing steps they never got to take together. But slowly, the pain transformed. His love for her never faded. It evolved. She was no longer just a memory he mourned. She became a presence he carried with him.

The years passed. Life moved forward, and so did Aaryan. But some things never changed. He never married. Never loved anyone else. He built a life for himself, but his heart remained loyal to the one love that had shaped him.

One evening, a few years after Maya's passing, Aaryan sat alone on the shores of Langkawi. The waves crashed gently against the sand, the wind carrying the scent of salt and freedom. For the first time in a long time, he smiled—softly, peacefully. And in that moment, he finally understood. Maya had never truly left him. She had never been confined to an urn, to a memory, to a place in the past. *She was here*. In the wind that brushed his face. In the sunlight that warmed his skin. In the stars that twinkled above him. And most of all—she was in his heart. *Forever.*

As the years passed, Aaryan's story became a quiet legend. People whispered about the man who traveled to Malaysia every year, retracing steps of a love that had defied time. Some called it tragic. Some called it beautiful. But for Aaryan, it was simply love—the kind that doesn't fade, doesn't die, but instead, finds a way to live on. Every year, on the same date, he would return to Malaysia.

And if you ever walked through the bustling streets of Kuala Lumpur on a certain day in the year, you might see a lone man standing by the Petronas Towers. He would gaze up at the sky, his lips parting to whisper one name.

Maya.

And if you listened carefully, you might hear the wind whisper back.

"I'm here."

*****

Connect with the Author

Thank you for reading! Stay connected and follow my journey:

📌 **Instagram:** @darshansingh0406
📌 **WhatsApp:** +91 – 8054045246
📌 **Email:** darshaman0406@gmail.com

I'd love to hear your thoughts! Leave a review or drop me a message.

📖 **Happy Reading!**